THE AMISH COWBOY'S LETTER

Large Print Edition

Amish Cowboys of Montana
Book 4

ADINA SENFT

Copyright 2023 by Shelley Adina Senft Bates

No part of this publication may be reproduced, distributed or transmitted in any form or by any means, including photocopying, recording, or other electronic or mechanical methods, without the prior written permission of the publisher, except in the case of brief quotations embodied in critical reviews and certain other noncommercial uses permitted by copyright law. For permission requests, write to the publisher at www.moonshellbooks.com.

This is a work of fiction. Names, characters, places, and incidents are a product of the author's imagination. Locales and public names are sometimes used for atmospheric purposes. Any resemblance to actual people, living or dead, or to businesses, companies, events, institutions, or locales is completely coincidental.

Cover design by Carpe Librum Book Design. Images used under license.

German quotations from the 1912 Luther Bible, with English from the King James Version. "Tell Me the Story of Jesus," lyrics by Fanny Crosby (1880), now in the public domain.

The Amish Cowboy's Letter / Adina Senft—1st large print ed.

ISBN 978-1-950854-65-3 R120324

 Created with Vellum

Praise for Adina Senft

"I got this book for my mother-in-law, but after I started reading a few paragraphs I couldn't put it down."

Robert A., Goodreads, on *The Amish Cowboy*

"The first thing I loved about this story is that it's set in Montana, so it was fun to shift gears from farming to ranching. The Montana landscape in winter is an added bonus! I also loved that this is a prequel to Senft's Montana Millers series, the origin story, if you will, of the Circle M Ranch. This story is a girl-next-door romance with layered characters and an overall sweetness to the tone that warms the heart."

Reading is My Superpower, on *The Amish Cowboy's Christmas*

"As with all this series, *The Amish Cowboy's Mistake* was fantastic. Adina Senft has a way of composing a storyline that not only holds your attention, but leaves you with a better outlook on your own faith, family, and overall perspective."

Cherese A., Goodreads, on *The Amish Cowboy's Mistake*

"Any book that can both entertain and leave me thinking is a book worth reading! Adina Senft is quickly becoming one of my favorite writers of Amish fiction.... Senft's characters are beautifully developed, [and] will move you to both laugh and cry."

Christian Fiction Addiction

In this series
AMISH COWBOYS OF MONTANA

The Amish Cowboy's Christmas prequel novella
The Amish Cowboy
The Amish Cowboy's Baby
The Amish Cowboy's Bride
The Amish Cowboy's Letter
The Amish Cowboy's Makeover
The Amish Cowboy's Home
The Amish Cowboy's Refuge
The Amish Cowboy's Mistake
The Amish Cowboy's Little Matchmakers
The Amish Cowboy's Wedding Quilt
The Amish Cowboy's Journey

I had many things to write, but I will not with ink and pen write unto thee:

    But I trust I shall shortly see thee, and we shall speak face to face.

3 John 1:13-14

THE AMISH COWBOY'S LETTER

Chapter 1
WHINBURG TOWNSHIP, PENNSYLVANIA

Circle M Ranch
Monday, May 17

Dear Elizabeth,

 I got your letter on Saturday but with Communion yesterday, there hasn't been time to answer until now. It's after nine and the family have all gone to bed, but Zach doesn't mind the lantern. We've been sharing a room all our lives and he's used to it.

 Friday afternoon Sara and I got called out by the volunteer fire department here. We jogged down to the end of the lane (a good half mile—keeps us in shape) and the EMT van picked us up. The fire truck had already gone over to Annie Gingerich's place. Remember I told you about her? Noah King, her great-nephew, is courting my sister Rebecca. Annie's the oldest member of the church here.

Anyway, the family were in town, and she was alone in the Daadi Haus when something on the stove caught fire. A neighbor saw the smoke and called 9-1-1, but by the time the truck got there, old Annie almost had it out. There is no moss on that woman, for sure and certain! She burned her left arm pretty bad, but luckily our Sara had a salve from Sarah Byler the Dokterfraa there in Whinburg Township. Our Sara went with her when they took her down to the hospital in Libby. You don't want to take chances with a sister that old. I went home and got the buggy and went in to Mountain Home to locate the Kings and let them know where she was.

On Saturday the hospital released Annie and now Sara goes over each day to check on her. With her EMT training and learning to be a Dokterfraa, the body of the church is well looked after in Mountain Home, ain't so?

Sunday, like I said, was Communion. It was the first time for my brother Joshua, Sara, and both my sisters since they were baptized last month, so it was pretty special. I wish you could have been there, and been part of the day with my family. There are times when missing you feels like a piece of me is gone. Part of it is remembering you—how sweet and beautiful you are, how just watching you walk down the road makes my heart jump. And part of it has been getting to know you in your letters. Especially in the last year. I believe we've really become something in the last year, haven't we?

I'm the family joke when it comes to getting the mail. Even my father has stopped expecting me to pay attention or finish what I'm doing the minute I hear Cathy the postal carrier's truck coming down the highway. It's kind of an old truck. Its engine is pretty distinctive. Sometimes I beat Cathy to the mailbox, and she just shakes her head at me and tells me whether or not there's a letter from you before she gives me the bundle.

Fact is, I'm not sure that letters are going to keep me going much longer. It's been almost two years since we met. I was on the back of the hay wagon helping our cousin Melvin take off his hay, and you leaned on the fence to ask if Carrie was home so you could order a cake. And that was it for me.

It still is. So … Elizabeth, if I were to send a train ticket, would you come to the ranch for a visit? It's time we saw each other again. I want you to see my life the way I was able to see yours. I want you to see Montana at its best, and love it as much as I do. My sisters will tell you there's nothing prettier than the Circle M in the early summer when the lupines are blooming.

I'll ask my mother to send a letter so that your parents know you'll be welcome, and Melvin and Carrie, of course, can tell them anything they need to know about us. I hope you'll think seriously about it. Because I am.

Your special friend and brother in Christ,
Adam

The Amish Cowboy's Letter

———

"YOU HAVE TO READ THIS." Kate Weaver held out Adam Miller's letter to her sister Elizabeth. Her hand shook just enough to make the paper tremble.

"Is that from Adam?" Elizabeth dropped the nightgown over her head and closed the window. Kate would get up after a while and open it—the smell of grass and flowers in the night air was *wunderbaar* to breathe as she dropped off to sleep. "It's so sweet of him to keep writing. You must be a far better correspondent than I ever was."

"Lizzie, I have to stop," Kate said a little desperately. "I can't go on writing your letters to him. I feel like I'm living a lie."

"No, you're not. I tell you what to write, mostly. I'm just not as good at it as you are, and my penmanship certainly isn't." Elizabeth sat on her own bed on the windowless side of the room, looking like one of the china angels Kate had seen in the gift store in Whinburg. Nobody could argue that when God was handing out the looks in the family, Elizabeth had been allowed back for seconds. With her rippling red-gold hair and long-lashed gray eyes, she had been turning boys' heads since they were scholars in the little schoolhouse down the road.

Not that looks mattered to an Amish woman, whose beauty was in her spirit and her faithful service to *Gmay und Gott*. But when it came to Adam Miller, Kate had wished more than once that her ordinary reddish-brown hair, dark blue eyes, and the freckles on her nose would be enough to get him to look her way.

Elizabeth yawned and pulled back the Carolina Lily quilt that Kate had made for her sixteenth birthday, with its green leaves and its blue and purple and burgundy flowers on a black ground. "Read me the important parts, okay?"

She always said that, and Kate always concealed a shiver of relief. Oh, she left the letters out in plain view in case Elizabeth ever did want to read them all the way through, but her sister never did, to Kate's knowledge. If she had, she would have seen sentences like, *There are times when missing you feels like a piece of me is gone.* Elizabeth was perfectly free to read Adam's beautiful words, if she cared to. But Kate was pretty sure she wouldn't.

That left Kate equally free to read those sentences over and over and pretend they were for her.

> Part of it has been getting to know you in your letters. Especially in the last year. I believe we've really become something in the last year, haven't we?

Yes, she did believe that. With all her heart.

There was one tiny little problem. Adam Miller didn't know that it was Kate writing Elizabeth's letters for her.

She did as Elizabeth asked, and read aloud the parts about the fire at Annie Gingerich's house, and his sisters and brother taking communion for the first time. Even the part about his wishing she was there.

Elizabeth groaned. "Okay, that's enough. It's clear that I'd better take matters into my own hands. *I wish you could have been there, and been part of the day with my family?* That sounds as if he's pretty serious, doesn't it?"

Kate bit back the urge to read his next precious sentence. Then she changed her mind. "He says right after that—

> There are times when missing you feels like a piece of me is gone. Part of it is remembering you. How sweet and beautiful you are. How just watching you walk down the road makes my heart jump. And part of it has been getting to know you through your letters."

Elizabeth sat up in bed and flung back the covers. "He said what? Give that to me."

Kate handed her the letter, feeling a prickle like acid across her shoulders and down her spine. She was found out. And yet, what a relief it would be not to have to do this anymore! To write to Adam as herself, and pour out her heart with her own name at the end!

By the time she reached the end of the letter, her sister's face looked flushed and incredulous in the lamplight.

"How on earth does he get all this from my

little bits of news?" Elizabeth glared at her. "What have you been telling him?"

"I—I—" Fifteen different answers crowded Kate's tongue, which meant none of them could come out.

"Kathryn Weaver, answer me."

Elizabeth was a year and a half younger than Kate, yet she sounded just like their Mammi Weaver when someone got into her raspberry jam.

"I told him your news," she said, trying to keep her voice steady and not like she was about to cry. "And maybe I ... embellished a little. He's so nice, Lizzie. He deserves something."

"He was the one who asked *me* to write, not the other way around. So have you told him about Mark and me?"

"*Neh,*" Kate mumbled to the top of the writing desk.

"We've been dating for six months, Kate! I told you last Christmas to put in something about Mark, so Adam would get the hint and stop writing. And now look!"

"I'm sorry," Kate faltered.

"I hope you are. You've made me look like a total flirt, and I'll look like a liar, too, if Mark—" She stopped.

Kate clutched at this straw, hoping it would deflect her sister's temper. "If Mark?"

"We've been talking," Elizabeth said. "About the future."

She drew in a breath. "Has he proposed?"

"*Neh,* but I think he might. My birthday is next week. I'll be twenty-one … and he's already asked if he can take me someplace special."

"Oh, Lizzie." She jumped up from the desk and flung her arms around her sister. "I'm so happy—he's such a good man. His sisters have told me that when he gets married, Eli Yoder will take him on as partner in the farm."

"I know." Elizabeth accepted the hug and Kate felt as though she could breathe again. She was forgiven.

"Elizabeth Yoder," Kate said, trying out the name on her tongue. "It suits you."

"It does, doesn't it?" Elizabeth climbed back under the covers and hugged her knees. "But let's not put the wagon before the horse. He hasn't asked me yet."

"My lips are sealed." Kate made a buttoning motion over her mouth.

"But you have to do something about Adam," Elizabeth went on without missing a beat. "Even if Mark doesn't propose, I suppose I've been wrong to keep up the correspondence. What's the good of a special friend on the other side of the country?" She twinkled at Kate. "There are plenty of nice boys here."

"Adam is nice," Kate said. Someone had to defend him.

"He is, but so is Cal Troyer. And Brian Detwiler already has his own farm."

"Good thing Mark isn't here to hear you say that," Kate said.

"If Mark were here, I'd have eyes for no one but him," Elizabeth said firmly. "I don't care about the others, not really. I think he's the one. Which is why Adam needs to understand that it's over—that it never really began. He absolutely can't send that ticket, or ask his mother to write. Or tell his mother anything at all, come to that. I know she writes to Carrie Miller." She paused, and her jaw firmed. "Can you do that, Kate? Without *embellishing* it and making it worse?"

The thought of having to write those words and hurt Adam sent a shard of grief through Kate's heart. *"Ja,"* she said at last. "I can do that."

"You'd better let me read it before you send it." Elizabeth slid down under the covers and pulled them up to her chin, as though they were in the deeps of January and not past the middle of May. "Promise?"

"I promise," Kate said.

The very words felt like rocks falling on her tender heart.

Even opening the window fifteen minutes later, when Elizabeth had dropped off to sleep, didn't help.

Chapter 2

Whinburg Township, Pennsylvania
May 21

Dear Adam,

Thank you for your letter. Your description of going out on the call to Annie Gingerich's house made my blood run cold. I'm so glad she is well looked after. I can imagine that the King family will be keeping a close eye on her and that stove, too. There comes a time when even the most independent person must accept help and ask someone from the family to move in.

We have been having a busy spring. My oldest brother visited with his wife and family for a couple of days to help Dad and my two younger brothers put in the crop. This year it's divided between corn and soybeans, both of which bring a good price. Already the corn is four inches high, and you can practically see the little bean plants wiggle as they stretch up for the sun. The vegetables that Kate and I helped Mom put in a couple of weeks ago are up and we're grateful for the rain. Just not too much! We have runner beans growing up on strings from the ground to the verandah roof on the south side of the house. It was Kate's idea, to see if it would give some shade in the heat of summer. Think how easy they'll be to pick. Just step outside and there you are. Dad says it will be Kate climbing out on the roof to prune them if they start growing into the eaves.

I know the growing season is short there in Montana, except, I guess, for cattle. What kinds of hardy vegetables does your mother plant? I would so like to see—

KATE STOPPED WRITING, horrified at herself. She had completely forgotten that she was supposed to be writing as Elizabeth. Supposed to be declining the offer of train tickets. She stared at the lines at the bottom of the sheet of lined notebook paper, wondering how to correct her mistake.

>—the Circle M in all its spring glory, but I can't. Like you, this is our busiest time of year, other than canning season at the end of summer. My mother can't manage without both Kate and me, and my youngest sister Anna May has two years left in school before she can really help with the heavy work. Thank you for the offer of the tickets, but Mom wouldn't let me accept them, or travel across the country alone. In fact—

"I can't do this," Kate whispered, laying down the ballpoint pen and covering her face with her hands. "*Mei Gott,* help me find the words."

Who could ever find the words to break a

man's heart? She ought to give this back to Lizzie and tell her to do it herself.

But Lizzie and Mark had taken the spring wagon to get calendula plants to keep the slugs out of the garden, and wouldn't be back before the mail came.

> —I've been giving a lot of thought to our correspondence, and much as I've enjoyed your letters, I wonder if being special friends over such a long distance is the right thing to do. I've become quite good friends with a young man here called Mark Yoder. I think you might have met him when you were here that summer. He's been taking me home from singing and my parents have made him welcome here at the farm.

She couldn't write that. It would hurt him so. But she had already written it. There was nothing for it but to finish as quickly as possible, and leave the letter out on the desk for her sister to read later. As promised.

Elizabeth had been spending Sundays with

the Yoders, had been going home from singing with Mark for months. In fact, he'd be staying for dinner tonight. She could already smell the savory scent of the roast wafting up the stairs from the kitchen. If she didn't hurry, she wouldn't get the cheese and rice casserole in the oven and she'd spoil Lizzie's carefully planned dinner.

> I hope you will forgive me. There must be a dozen girls in Montana who would jump at the chance for a ride home from singing with you, Adam. I don't mean to hurt you, and I hope you will understand. Sometimes our hearts change with the seasons of life, the way the leaves on the trees change.

Dead leaves, falling when there is no hope left of sustenance. She had to finish. Quickly, like ripping off a bandage strip.

> I wish you every blessing God has in store for you.
> Your sister in Christ,
> Elizabeth

Feeling as though she'd wounded him just as deeply as if he'd been standing here in the room, she pushed the letter away.

Then she put her head down on her arms and cried as though it were her own heart she'd just broken.

———

KATE HAD KNOWN Mark Yoder all her life. He had been two grades above her in school, four above Elizabeth, and had been the kind of boy who would rather be outside playing some kind of sport, even in the rain and snow, than inside playing games when the weather was bad.

But now, Kate had to admit, that preference would probably serve him well. Farmers didn't get to stay inside if it meant getting the crop in the ground or finishing harvest before the rain started.

Her thoughts drifted—again—to Adam and his family on the Circle M. Adam had written about calving season, about haying season, even about Christmas, when the work slowed and the Miller cowboys stayed in the barn, fixing equipment and repairing tack, getting ready to do it all over again the next year. He had written about the camaraderie in the tack room, about the jokes around the dinner table—even when they were on him. There were plenty of jokes and companionship in her family, too, but the simple fact that Adam was there made it seem more appealing. How *wunderbaar* it would be to share simple pleasures knowing that he was only a glance away.

Elizabeth nudged her with an elbow to her ribs, and Kate blinked herself back to the dinner table and real life.

"Mamm, Dat, everyone … Mark and I have something to tell you." She got up and went around the table to where he sat on Dat's left hand, in the guest's place.

What happened to the special dinner? He couldn't wait? was Kate's first thought. Her second was, *I'll have to rewrite that letter—and it was hard enough the first time.*

Mark stood, took Elizabeth's hand, and turned toward Mamm and Dat respectfully. "This afternoon I asked Elizabeth to marry me, and she said yes," he said.

This afternoon? Surely he hadn't asked her on the highway, rattling along in the spring wagon, or at Corinne and Isaac Yoder's place, where they were getting the started plants. No, if Elizabeth wasn't to have her romantic dinner, then surely they must have gone somewhere special for such a moment. No wonder they'd been late getting back.

Their two younger sisters squealed and clutched each other's hands, bouncing in their seats.

Dat pushed back his chair and shook Mark's hand heartily. "I can't say I didn't see this coming. I'm happy for the two of you," he said.

Mamm hugged Elizabeth and then Mark, while Kate and their sisters engulfed Elizabeth in a joyful many-armed hug. "Have you picked a date?"

"We have to check with the bishop," Mark said, "but I'm hoping for early November, or maybe even late October. That way, we'll be able to enjoy Christmas together, and make our honeymoon visits before plowing starts in March."

"And I understand your father is taking you on as partner?" Dat asked casually.

Mark nodded. "He is, and he's selling me a section of land." Dat's eyebrows went up. They hadn't known that. "Once the papers are signed, we'll stay temporarily in the *Daadi Haus* while we build our own place."

"How exciting," Mamm said, her eyes sparkling. "You'll live right here in our own district, and we can see each other regularly, even at church."

"That's the best part." Elizabeth, who rarely showed emotion, positively glowed. "I don't think I could stand to marry someone from far away, and only get to see my family once a year at most." She glanced at Kate, then back to Mamm. "My husband, my home, and my life will be right here in Whinburg Township, where we both belong."

Our home. Our life. But Kate shook her head at herself for picking at pronouns. This was all new to Elizabeth. It would probably take a while to think of herself as part of a *we* rather than simply an *I*.

"Thanks be to the *gut Gott* for that," Dat said.

"Let us bow our heads now, and give a word of thanks to Him from whom all blessings flow."

"And then we'll have dessert?" Kate's youngest brother asked as everyone resumed their seats around the table.

"Prayer first, then dessert," Mamm said firmly.

Afterward, Kate and the younger girls got up to clear. Elizabeth stood, too, but Kate nudged her into her seat again. "We'll get this. We want to hear all about your plans."

For a person who had only been engaged for two hours, Elizabeth had a lot of plans to share. It was clear to the point of blushes and giggles that she had been thinking of this for a long time—maybe even since the first date. Even Mark had to laugh at how prepared she was.

He accepted a piece of strawberry shortcake and whipped cream from Mamm and gave the plate to Elizabeth, waiting for the next one for himself. "I have to say, I love a woman who plans ahead," he told her, gazing into her eyes. "Leave the hymns to me, is all I ask."

"Done," she said, and popped a choice strawberry into his mouth. "Would you prefer lavender and cream as our colors, or royal blue and white?"

"I don't even know what lavender is," he complained, and everyone laughed.

"All you need to know is that whatever Elizabeth chooses, it will be beautiful," Kate said. Which was the unvarnished truth. Lizzie had a gift for creating beauty around her. It didn't hurt that she was so pretty herself that she always fit in.

That night, after family prayers and after Mark had gone, Elizabeth was still glowing with happiness. But there was one thing still left to do before Kate could have any hope of sleeping tonight.

"I wrote the letter," she said, indicating the sheets of notebook paper on the desk. "You said you wanted to read it before I sent it."

"What letter?" Elizabeth picked it up and glanced through the opening paragraphs. "Oh. To Adam." She folded it in neat thirds and laid it down. "You told him I was engaged, *nix*?"

"I didn't know until supper. So, *neh*."

"I don't suppose it matters. As long as you

said it was over and I wasn't coming, that's the main thing."

"I did, Lizzie." Kate's cheeks burned. "I wrote just what you said."

"No embellishments?"

"*Neh.*"

"*Gut.*" She climbed under the Carolina Lily quilt. "What are you making for our wedding present?"

"Lizzie! You'll just have to wait and see." The truth was, she was going to make another quilt, but for some reason she hadn't seen or thought of a design just yet. It would take some careful consideration of color and pattern.

"If it's a quilt, can it be in the Mariner's Compass pattern? Like the one I saw over at the Beilers' place last church Sunday."

The Mariner's Compass. Well, at least it was an easier pattern than a Double Wedding Ring. "Any preference about the colors?"

"Not pink."

Kate stopped braiding her hair. "Who makes a quilt for a married couple that's pink?"

"I'm just making sure," her sister said, unperturbed, and Kate resumed braiding.

"Ideally, though, wouldn't it be beautiful if it were in our wedding colors?"

"When you decide on them."

"It could have a royal blue heart, shading out to lavender on the points," Elizabeth said dreamily. "Then I could have all my favorite colors and not have to choose."

Could made it sound as if this was only one of many possibilities, but Kate knew her sister. "It sounds beautiful," she said. "I can't wait to get started."

Elizabeth went on, "I wonder if we could have royal blue and lavender napkins, so I don't have to choose there, either."

And that was that, as far as Kate was concerned. Decision made.

The next day, Kate's head was full of colors and combinations of shades as she did her chores while working out the quilt design in her head. That was the beauty of weeding the vegetable garden. Not only did she get to consider the variations of the blues in Mamm's bearded iris, she could think about whether any shades of green could be worked in to give the quilt a more varied look. And there were so many kinds of Mariner's Compass, too—maybe she'd better walk over to Paul and Barbara Byler's and take a close look at the one that had attracted Elizabeth's attention. The last thing she wanted was for Elizabeth to express her gratitude on her wedding day, and then not use the quilt because it was the wrong pattern. Kate had seen her do that before, when they were younger. She'd asked for a particular puzzle for her eleventh birthday. She'd received a puzzle, but it wasn't the one she'd specified. The next thing Kate knew, their sisters were putting it together, and she never did see Elizabeth working on it.

But, she supposed, when you were creating beauty around you, it wasn't made of any old thing. It was specific. Except for the things the *gut Gott* had made, of course.

What did Mark plan to give her for an engagement gift? Kate didn't dare ask.

Surely anything the man she loved gave her would be perfect.

After lunch she walked up the lane to put the letter to Adam in the box. As much as she wanted to rewrite it, she wanted it on its way even more. And just as though *Gott* was making sure she didn't chicken out and not mail it at all, here came the postal delivery truck, rattling up the slope toward her. She handed the letter through the passenger window and got a thick bundle in return. The postal carrier waved and drove on while she walked slowly back up the lane and sorted through the collection. A fat circle letter for Mamm, whose buddy bunch traded quilt patterns and seed packets with equal enthusiasm from their homes scattered all over Pennsylvania and Ohio. A couple of business letters for Dat, and some bills. An issue of *The Budget,* and a letter addressed to Mamm in a neat but unfamiliar hand.

But the return address in the corner was as familiar to Kate as her own name.

N. Miller,
Circle M Ranch,
R.R. 4 Mountain Home, Montana

Adam's mother's name was Naomi.

Kate sucked in a breath. There was only one reason Naomi would be writing to Mamm. *I'll ask my mother to send a letter so that your parents know you'll be welcome.*

He hadn't even waited to hear back from Elizabeth before he'd gone ahead and done what he said he would. But in just a few days, Adam would receive the letter meant to let him down easy. The one she'd just seen drive away. Oh dear.

Kate had nearly reached the house, in a daze of apprehension, when she realized one last detail about the envelope she had to hand over to her mother. It was too thick for an ordinary one-page letter. Thick, and a bit stiff.

As though there was something else inside. Like a train ticket.

She closed her eyes, and right there in the yard, sent up a prayer for strength. Moments like this were why Amish women wore the *Kapp*—the prayer covering. Because you never knew when or how many times a day you were going to need to pray for God's help.

Chapter 3

TAKING A DEEP BREATH, Kate went into the kitchen and handed Mamm the mail.

"*Denki*, Kate." Mamm riffled through it. "Ach, *gut*, my circle letter! And what's this?"

She slit it open with her thumb while Kate's stomach did a flip. "That's from Naomi Miller in Montana. Her husband is a first cousin of Melvin Miller, over the creek on the other side of Whinburg."

Mamm glanced at her. "You're well informed, aren't you?"

"Lizzie was writing to Naomi's son Adam for a while."

Mamm read the single page in one hand, holding the ticket in the other. Then she handed the letter to Kate, her face slack with astonishment. "I feel like I'm reading a letter meant for someone else. Do you know anything about this?"

Dear Ellie Weaver,

My son Adam has asked me to write to you to ask if your daughter Elizabeth might come for a visit. They've been corresponding as special friends for some time, he tells me. We live on a ranch in northwestern Montana, but they met the summer before last, when he was helping our cousins Carrie and Melvin Miller with chores on the farm. Melvin was traveling with the auction crew, if I remember right, and they needed help getting the crop in.

Rest assured that your daughter will be well looked after. If she comes before Memorial Day, maybe she'd like to ride out with our family when we take the cattle up to the summer pastures. It's always a big event, and the more helpers the better. We feed the crew breakfast before they go up and when they get back, there's a big barbecue and all the neighbors who have helped stay for supper. It's a lot of fun, and Adam would be so pleased to see her join in.

I'm enclosing a one-way train ticket from Lancaster to Libby. Adam assures me that Elizabeth already knows it's coming, but he wanted me to write to you, too, so you know everything is above board. If you're nervous about her traveling alone, you're very welcome to send a sister or brother with her. We have lots of room here.

We look forward to meeting Elizabeth. If you have any questions, I know Carrie Miller will be happy to tell you anything you need to know about us all. It would be faster than a letter.

Your brethren in Christ,
Reuben and Naomi Miller

Kate felt sick. This was getting worse and worse. She had to tell Mamm the truth, before the latter hitched up the buggy horse and went over to Carrie Miller's to demand an explanation. Then Kate's shameful secret would be out, and would for sure and certain get back to Adam before she could figure out a way to make this right.

"*Ja*," she said hoarsely. "I know a little of how this came about."

"Maybe you'd like to let me in on the secret?" Mamm took the letter from Kate's limp fingers and sat down at the kitchen table, reading it again as though it might say something different this time. "How can Elizabeth be writing to a boy in Montana when she's engaged to Mark Yoder? What kind of a *Dochsder* have I raised?"

"It's not Elizabeth's fault," Kate said desperately. "It's mine." She pulled out a chair and reached into the pocket of her kitchen apron. Thank goodness she had a tissue—used and crumpled, but it would do.

"How can it be your fault? You didn't exactly write Elizabeth's letters for her."

"That's the trouble, Mamm." She dragged a breath into her lungs. "I did. I mean, I have been. For about eighteen months."

Her mother stared at her. "I don't

understand. And you'd better tell me quick, before the *Kinner* come in from school."

Dear Father, help me find the words.

Begin at the beginning. That was always best. "Two years ago, like Naomi Miller says, they met and when Adam went back to Montana, they started a correspondence."

Her mother nodded. "I remember."

"But Lizzie, well, you know her. She'll date a boy for a while, then someone else will catch her eye and she'll date him. Or them both."

"That's an awful thing to say about your sister, Kathryn Weaver."

"I don't mean it to be awful," Kate wailed, tears welling in her eyes at her mother's tone. "It's just the way she is. Was. And then she started seeing Mark, and all that changed. No other man would do for her."

"Except this young man Adam, out in Montana. Are you getting to that part?"

Kate swiped at her eyes with the tissue. "*Ja.* You know how much trouble Lizzie had in school with learning to read, and penmanship lessons. How we used to spend extra time in the evening, helping her."

"When she was little. What does that have to do with her now?"

"She got better, but she was never comfortable with writing letters. Christmas cards and recipes, no problem, but anything more? I used to help her with the letters to Adam. With words. Spelling. Things to write about. After about six months, she just kind of … gave up. Because it was hard for her. But she still liked Adam, so she asked me to help her still. She'd tell me what she wanted to say, and I'd write the letter."

"You shouldn't have done that, Kate. A person's correspondence is private."

"Not this correspondence," Kate said wryly. "We'd been doing it together since the beginning."

Mamm huffed and shook her head. "What I don't understand is how she could lead the poor boy on when she had no intention of going any further."

"That … might be my fault."

Mamm stared at her. Waiting.

"After she started dating Mark, Lizzie mostly lost interest in it. Of course she did. She had a real boyfriend, not a long-distance one who was just a memory. Every time I answered one of Adam's letters, I knew I had to tell him. This time I would, I'd say to myself. But ... I didn't have the heart." She swallowed, and met her mother's gaze. "His letters are wonderful, Mamm. So descriptive. Deep. He really thinks about things—work on the ranch, making it more profitable, his relationships with his family, his walk with God. I—I wrote to him like a friend."

"Like a special friend, if this train ticket is any indication."

Mamm was no slouch at putting two and two together.

Kate hung her head, her *Kapp* strings swinging forward. "That was where I sinned. I forgot to write as Elizabeth and began to write as myself."

"Ach, Dochsder." Mamm slipped an arm around her shoulders and squeezed. "Whatever next? Have you even met this boy in person?"

"He's not a boy. He's twenty-four—two years older than me. And yes, he ran around with the *Youngie* when he was here. Since I was usually with Elizabeth, I saw a fair bit of him. I—I liked him. And Mamm, he's been baptized since he visited."

As though he was getting his life in order. Preparing himself to be a husband. For Elizabeth.

Kate's lips trembled at the magnitude of what she had done. What she had allowed Lizzie to do.

Mamm sighed, gazing at the letter on the table. "How am I going to write to this woman? I should just hand this to Elizabeth and tell her to deal with it."

She had never dealt with it before.

"It's not likely she will," Kate said cautiously. "But I wrote—um, sent—a letter just now to Adam. That's why I was out at the mailbox. I ... let him down easy. Told him she was seeing someone."

"She's doing more than seeing Mark, Kate. They're going to the bishop, probably this week."

"I know, I know. But he's going to be so hurt. What else could I do?"

"Tell him the truth. Set him free, like the Scriptures say."

"I will," she promised. "In the next letter."

"Honestly, I don't know who I'm more disappointed in—you or Elizabeth. Playing with this young man's feelings for so long. I don't understand it. Not one bit."

"If you read his letters you might," Kate offered.

"I think his privacy has been toyed with quite enough." Mamm got up. "I'll show this to Elizabeth and tell her to write to him. Even if it's only two lines, she's got to do it. This has to end now, before Mark hears about it."

Kate nodded, stuffed the damp tissue back in her pocket, and fled outside to the garden.

Her younger siblings were coming up the lane, chattering and horsing around. The tomato plants hid her from their sight, nodding around her, green and scented and promising hope of food for later in the summer. Already recovering from the hoeing she'd given them earlier.

But it would take her a lot longer to recover from the loss of Adam's letters. She'd never see him again, yet her mistake would always be a part of him, the way a broken bone was always a part of you.

Hidden from view of the house by the tomato plants, Kate knelt in the soil and wept for a secret, wonderful dream that now would never come true.

A BUGGY RATTLED up the lane, and Kate wiped her face with her apron, since the tissue was too damp to do any good. She straightened enough to peer over the fuzzy leaves, already starred with yellow blossoms, then stood. Elizabeth had gone in to Whinburg to the stationery store, to begin looking over their stock of wedding invitations. Once she'd narrowed her favorites down to two, she'd ask Mark to pick the one he liked.

It did not look as though the initial search had gone well. Elizabeth jumped out of the buggy in front of the barn doors, her step as close to stomping as Kate had ever seen.

"Lizzie," she called. "How did it go?"

"There you are. I have a bone to pick with you. Help me with the horse."

Uh-oh. Had she gone into the fabric store, too, and found that they didn't stock the colors she wanted in her quilt? Miriam Beiler over in Willow Creek probably did—her shop window was a delight when new fabrics came in, especially now, in the early summer. But why would that cause a bone of contention between them?

Together, they unhitched the buggy horse and turned her out into the pasture, where she kicked up her heels and galloped over to exchange news with the other horses. Kate closed the gate and turned to her sister.

"All right," she said. "What's wrong? Did something happen in town?"

"I'll say it did. I bumped into Carrie Miller outside the bakery and made the mistake of asking her about a cake. I didn't mention it was for my wedding."

"Why would that be a mistake?" Everyone knew that Carrie had a masterful touch with cakes for special occasions, almost like a gift from God. "You haven't set a date yet, but

November is ages away. Is she booked up already?"

"Not yet, but that's not the point. Imagine how I felt asking her for a fancy white cake, only to find out she thought it was for my wedding to Adam!"

Kate drew in a shuddering breath and covered her mouth with her fingers. *"Ach, neh."*

"What am I going to do, Kate? What if Mark gets wind of it?"

"Hopefully he knows the truth."

"That is not funny."

"I wasn't joking. Honestly, Lizzie, I don't know what could have happened. I sent Adam a letter this afternoon saying you were seeing someone else."

"I'm not *seeing* Mark—I'm engaged to him!"

"I meant to let him down easy," Kate said lamely, for the second time today.

"That's not good enough. If his family here in the township thinks he's that serious, what are they going to think of me when Mark and I announce our engagement?"

"You won't do that for months."

Elizabeth glared at her.

Kate had better tell Elizabeth what had come in the mail. "You're not going to like this, but Adam's mother wrote to Mamm and sent a train ticket for you."

"What?"

The horses tensed at Elizabeth's shriek, and trotted to the far corner of the pasture as a precautionary measure.

"Do you think his mother wrote to Carrie at the same time?" Elizabeth groaned and covered her face with her hands. "I bet she did. Why else would Carrie come right out with an assumption like that?"

"I don't know."

"Did Mamm read it?"

"Oh, *ja*. An hour ago."

"What did she say?"

"Pretty much what you're saying."

"Come on." Elizabeth grabbed her wrist. "You have to fix this mess you've got me into."

There was no point in protesting the injustice of this. Blame lay on both sides, but there was no point in sending Elizabeth around the bend by pointing it out.

They found Mamm in the kitchen mixing

cookie dough. The *Kinner* were out in barn and henhouse doing their after-school chores. Elizabeth snatched up the letter and when she'd read it, streaks of color rode high in her cheeks. Rapidly, she told Mamm about meeting Carrie in town. She ended with, "What am I going to do, Mamm? The whole family is going to despise me for leading Adam on when I didn't. Kate did."

"It's a pickle, all right," Mamm said mildly. "But you have to get yourself out of it. Go upstairs right now and write Adam the truth. Your letter will only be a day behind the one Kate wrote for you—and with any luck, hers will get stuck somewhere and yours will arrive first."

"I should just telephone him."

"You have their number?" Kate said in surprise.

"I have Adam's number. He's on the volunteer fire crew, so he has a separate phone he shares with Sara."

Kate had just begun to feel a trickle of relief that this ordeal might be over that easily, when Mamm shook her head. "You are not going to use the phone shanty for that. It's for necessities and emergencies, *Dochsder*."

Elizabeth groaned. "Mamm, if this isn't an emergency, I don't know what is."

"It's unkind, is what it is. A woman can't say something like this over the phone. Think of how hurt he will be."

"If he is, it's because Kate wrote those things to him."

"What's done is done," Mamm chided her. "You'll write your letter tonight. No need to be flowery. Just tell the truth. And don't do it now. Write it later, when you've had time to calm down."

"*Neh*," Elizabeth said. "Kate got me into this. Kate can write it."

Today's effort had been difficult enough to bring her to tears. How would she ever find the words to write anything as brutal as the truth? "*Ach, neh,* Lizzie—" Kate began.

Mamm cut her off with a wave of the mixing spoon.

"*You* will write it," she told Elizabeth in the tone they both knew meant no argument.

"I won't," Elizabeth said, her grey eyes

stormy and the color surging back into her face. "Kate's the one who's in love with him. She can write as herself for once. And tell him what she's done."

"Elizabeth!" Mamm exclaimed, clearly as shocked as Kate was to hear such words spoken aloud, and in anger to boot.

And suddenly, as though *Gott* himself put the solution into her mind, Kate knew what she had to do. Maybe Elizabeth was right. Maybe she wasn't. But Adam deserved to hear this news from someone who cared, at least. Someone he'd come to know as a friend.

"I'll do it," she said. "But not in a letter, or over the phone. He needs to know everything. About what I did. About Elizabeth's choice." She looked her mother in the eye. "I'll take that train ticket to Montana, and tell him in person."

Chapter 4
MOUNTAIN HOME, MONTANA

May 28

NO ANSWER HAD COME to the letter Adam sent Elizabeth ten days ago. Ten days of silence, without so much as a hint of what might be going through her mind. Had he been too forward? Had Mamm's letter enclosing the ticket frightened her off? Despite her letters, was she not ready to take the next step? If she didn't want to write anymore, why didn't she call what Sara termed the "fire phone" to let him know?

He'd given her the number, and she'd never

used it. But her letters had more than made up for it. Until now.

Not for the first time this week, Adam's stomach soured and he felt almost sick.

He and Joshua were coming down the mountain from their allotment seven miles away from the ranch. On Monday, their neighbors would gather before sunup and help to trail the cattle along the highway and through the gates, then up to the high meadows. The cattle would feed in the summer pastures, getting sleek and fat for market in the fall. Their job today was to check the gates and fences so that the cattle would be directed to the right places at each stage of the day-long trip.

It wasn't demanding work, but they had to keep their wits about them. One fence post down or some barbed wire broken, and a calf might take off through the gap and fall prey to a coyote or be hit by a passing vehicle. The calves were too valuable to let that happen. But still, thoughts of Elizabeth had intruded all day, and last night in camp he'd dreamed about her.

Now, in the clear, not-yet-warm light of the spring morning, as he and Joshua turned in at the Circle M gate, he'd almost convinced himself that he'd offended her so badly he would never hear from her again.

As they approached the house, the front door opened, light spilling down the stairs and showing them a slender female figure clattering down, as though she had something urgent to say.

Delphinium blew a breath as though impatient to be in her warm stall, but Adam pulled up, the volunteer fireman in him on alert, his saddle leather creaking. "Are we called out?" That was the only explanation he could think of. It was six in the morning, but that didn't mean anything. Accidents never happened when it was convenient.

"*Neh.*" It was Sara, waving the fire phone in one hand. "A girl just called. She's at the bus station in Mountain Home and needs a ride out here."

Something slammed into his stomach and snatched his breath.

"A girl?" Josh asked his fiancée. "What girl?"

"The one Adam's been writing to, I think." Sara's face crinkled up in apology while Adam's heartbeat took off at a gallop. "I'm so sorry—I thought it was a call-out and by the time I realized she was Amish and healthy and all she needed was a ride, I completely forgot the name she said and just told her someone would be there in half an hour. Reuben is hitching up the buggy."

"It's Elizabeth." A miracle, straight from *Himmel*. "Elizabeth Weaver is at the bus station. Why in creation didn't she let us know she was coming today?"

"You'll have to ask her," Sara said in her practical fashion. "Sorry for not getting her name. I'm good in a crisis … but when it's not a crisis I guess I need some practice."

Adam swung down off Del as he heard the barn door slide open. "It's okay, Sara. Josh, can you look after Del? I'm taking that buggy into town."

"Can't wait to see your girl, huh?" Josh grinned at him. *"Mei Bruder,* you smell like a cow pie. Nice first impression." But he took Del's reins, clearly able to see that Adam was in no mood for horsing around and jokes.

"Naomi and the twins are getting the guest

room ready," Sara said. "And I'll set another place for breakfast." The family had been expecting them home before daylight—but not that company would be arriving at the same time.

He practically took Hester's reins out of Dat's hands as his father was about to climb into the buggy, and assured him that he'd collect their not-quite-expected guest.

"I don't mind going to get her," Dat said mildly. "Sure you don't want to get cleaned up first?"

But Adam shook his head and clambered in. If Elizabeth was waiting in the bus station at this hour, no power on earth would prevent him from fetching her, no matter what he smelled like. Besides, she knew he worked on the family ranch—and even if he didn't, there weren't too many Amish women who were strangers to cow pies.

The five miles to town went past in a blur of ranch land and pine trees he'd watched grow all his life, with the image of Elizabeth superimposed on it all like a vision. "I can't believe it," he said. "I just can't believe she came all that way without a word of warning. She must have left as soon as she got the ticket." Hester's ear swivelled toward him as she trotted at her easy, long-legged pace down the highway. "If she left Lancaster on Monday, she'd have had to transfer in Pittsburgh and Chicago." He knew the route from having traveled it two years ago, in a daze of love that agonized over every mile, every whistle stop the train put between them. "If she got to Libby at midnight, did she spend the night in the station? The first bus doesn't leave until five."

But Hester had no reply.

When they reached the town limits, people were just beginning to stir, making coffee, getting ready to go to work. The small bus station was on the far side of what passed for a downtown in Mountain Home, made more prosperous lately by the Amish families who had moved to the district and opened businesses here. He counted off the quilt shop, the candle shop, the *Englisch* bookstore, the Yoders' variety store, the blacksmith and tack shop run by Alden Stolzfus … and there was the bar where Sara had walked in just before

Christmas last year and found Joshua with a baby in a basket.

She'd walked in from the bus station, right next door. Now, he could see an Amish girl sitting on a bench outside the glass-and-steel door, a carry-on sized suitcase with wheels at her feet. Not Elizabeth, he saw at a glance. But not anyone from here, either. He hoped her party wouldn't keep her waiting long.

He looped the reins over the rail in the three-sided buggy shed in the parking lot that kept the weather off the horses, and jogged over to the door, already straining for his first sight of the girl who had haunted his dreams for months.

He pushed the door halfway open and stopped. There was no one there except a yawning *Englisch* man behind the ticket counter. Maybe she was in the restroom. Maybe he should ask—

"Adam?" The girl sitting on the bench stood.

He dragged his focus off the waiting room to take her in, and let the door swing closed. She was tall, but not thin. Dark green dress with a black cape and apron, like they wore in

Lancaster County. Black hand-knitted sweater. Black away bonnet. And in its depths a heart-shaped face with a freckled nose, and eyes of a blue so deep they reminded him of the mountain gentians they sometimes found blooming in sheltered spots on the south side of a slope.

She looked vaguely familiar.

Was that how she knew his name? Had they met somewhere?

"I'm Adam Miller," he said. "I'm sorry—I'm picking someone up. Have you seen a strawberry blonde wearing a Lancaster County *Kapp*? She called for a ride and I came as soon as I could."

"That was me," the girl said. "I called the number Elizabeth gave me. She said it was the fire phone. I hope that was all right."

He stared at her, not understanding a word. Except for the name. He heard the name like a bell struck inside him.

"You know Elizabeth? Did you come with her?" Of course she had. What *ein Narr* she must think he was! "Is she in the bathroom? Does she have a suitcase? I can put both of them in the buggy."

"*Neh.*" The girl swallowed. "She's not here."

"Is she getting coffee? I don't think the café is open until seven—"

"No, I mean, she's still in Whinburg Township. She didn't come. I came instead. I'm her sister, Kate Weaver."

Her words pattered on his ears, containing no meaning whatsoever.

"I don't understand."

"I came instead of her."

That did not clear up the situation.

"I'm sorry I used your ticket without telling you. But I—it wasn't something you could say over the phone. And letters have caused this whole problem—I mean, my writing has—so I thought—"

"Wait." He put both hands up as though wasps were swarming around his ears. "Stop. Are you telling me Elizabeth didn't come?"

"*Ja.*"

"Is she coming later?"

"*Neh.*"

"Just you?"

"*Ja.*"

He gazed at her helplessly. "Mind telling me why it's you and not her?"

She gulped and took a deep breath. "This is all my fault. So I felt it was only right that I come and tell you in person." She looked around at the utilitarian bus station, the parking lot. Took in the Old West era buildings across the street. Then looked up, and her expression became tinged with awe as the sun broke over the mountains and lit the valley with golden light.

She blinked as he realized he was still standing there. Still waiting for her to tell him what came after *but*. "Is there somewhere a little less public we could go?"

"Well, I can't leave you here. The next bus back to Libby isn't until noon." He hooked a thumb over his shoulder. "We might as well go home. You can tell me what this is all about on the way."

She bit her lip at his tone and ratcheted the handle out of the suitcase, to follow him meekly to the buggy. He lifted her bag into the back and untied Hester while she climbed in. He could see her clutching her handbag and taking in the town as they clip-clopped through it. Alden Stolzfus turned in the act of unlocking the shop door, and lifted a hand in a wave as they rolled past. Adam was too distracted to even think to wave back.

A few more minutes took them out of town and on to the highway, with its wide shoulders that accommodated the buggies of the Amish. He glanced at the girl he barely remembered before he turned his attention back to the road. "All right," he said. "How about you start at the beginning. You have five miles to get to the end."

She took a deep, shuddering breath. "The first thing I want you to understand is how very sorry I am. I never should have started it. If I hadn't been so— Well, never mind."

After a moment, he prompted, "The beginning?"

"*Ja*. Sorry. Since she was a little scholar, Elizabeth has had trouble with writing things. She gets words mixed up, almost as though she's not seeing them properly. So all of us have helped her, me especially. We used to do exercises together after supper to help her write her vocabulary words."

Maybe he ought to have been more specific about where the beginning actually began.

"So when you wrote to her," Kate went on, "answering your letters was quite difficult for her."

"You could have fooled me."

She made a sound halfway between a gulp and a whimper. "I'm getting to that. As I said, when you began writing to her, I would help her with her words, and she would write back. Then I'd help her with whole sentences, if she couldn't think of anything to say. She'd write them down—practice, you know—so the hard words would come out properly. Each letter took two or three tries. Finally she kind of gave up, and asked if she could stand next to the desk and just tell me what to say."

With a sense of horror, Adam wondered if there had been anything in those early letters that a sister couldn't read. Not that there was a blessed thing he could do about it now. But still, something inside him smarted at discovering what he had believed to be private between himself and the girl he had fallen so hard for … wasn't.

When he couldn't say anything, she went on, "As the months passed, I began to enjoy writing her letters to you. Sometimes she didn't have much to put in, so I wrote as if—as if—" She choked, and cleared her throat. "As if you were writing to me."

His hands jerked on the reins, and Hester turned her head to look at him, startled. He made a soothing noise and shook them more gently to put her back on her pace. "That was wrong," he managed.

"I know. But—but—oh, please forgive me, Adam. Your letters were wonderful. I felt as though you were sharing your world with me."

"I was sharing it with *Elizabeth*."

A quick inhale, as though his words had struck a blow. "I know. I was wrong. So was she. We were both wrong to deceive you."

He was in no mood for apologies, no mood to hear her say a word against Elizabeth when it was she, Kate, who by her own admission had done the deceiving.

"So tell me this," he said roughly. "Was any of

it the truth? The tone—the words—they made me believe she cared. That if I sent a ticket, she would come. Was all that a lie, too?"

"Ja," she whispered. "At least—that was my mistake. My sin. I have to tell you something hard now. Did you get my—her—last letter?"

"I haven't had a letter since I wrote ten days ago. From either of you."

"Oh," she said in surprise. And not a nice surprise, either. The kind of surprise a man got when he shook his boot in the morning and a scorpion fell out. "I can't believe I beat it here. Oh, dear."

"We have two miles to go." And if she didn't tell him what she was getting at, he'd leave her here on the side of the road. She could walk back to town.

"The truth is—" Her throat closed again. "The truth is that she's engaged, Adam. To a man called Mark Yoder. They've been to the bishop and they'll be getting married on the last Thursday in October."

A cold shower of shock rendered him speechless. His hands went loose on the reins, and Hester slowed to an uncertain stop. She looked over her shoulder at him again, got no response, and lowered her head to crop the grass on the wayside.

"I'm so sorry," Kate said. He could hear the tears in her voice, but he could not look at her.

He saw only a vision of Elizabeth and some faceless man called Mark Yoder standing up in front of the *Gmay*, both in new clothes made especially for the momentous occasion, the bishop looking from one to the other as they said their vows.

As *Elizabeth* said her vows. To a man who was not him.

From somewhere far away, he heard someone weeping. Perhaps it was himself. But *neh*, his eyes were dry. Clear. He could feel the grief beginning to build, though. The tears wrung from a faithful man who had held his heart out to a woman for safekeeping. He felt as though she had slapped it from his hands, and the best gift he had to give lay on the ground, still beating.

Rejected. Unwanted. Stepped on.

A car passed them in the other lane, the

driver laying on the horn, as if they were blocking his way.

Hester threw up her head and sidled toward the ditch, and instinctively he grasped the reins and let her know he was still with her, still in control. He shook them, and the buggy jerked as they rolled on. One more curve, and they'd see the fence marking the Circle M land.

Home.

He'd deposit Kate Weaver with his mother. He'd put Hester in the barn and rub her down. Then he'd take himself off to his special place, where no one would find him unless he let them. And there he would stay until he could face the world again.

The way it felt now, he'd be building a hermit's lean-to and staying there for good.

Chapter 5

NOW KATE KNEW what a piece of luggage felt like in the belly of the bus, with no one there to claim it.

Adam had taken her into the kitchen of the big ranch house, introduced her to his mother and sisters in the briefest terms possible, and gone out to unhitch the horse. When his brothers and his father came in after washing up, he was not among them. Something inside her clenched with regret and hurt. He was unable to face his family, and it was her fault.

Reuben Miller counted heads in a rapid

glance. "Where is Adam? I saw him looking after Hester. He can't still be out there."

"I'll get him." A young man close to Adam's age loped out the back door. Zach.

Adam had written quite a lot about him—they were the boys in the middle and were close. Their eldest brother was Daniel, who after his recent wedding had moved with his bride and her son into the new house he had built on the far side of the river meadows. The youngest son was Joshua, and that must be Sara next to him, nuzzling the *Boppli* he held to make the infant laugh. Nathan, that was the *Boppli*'s name. And here were Rebecca and Malena, the twins who couldn't have looked less like twins if they'd tried. One was blond and quiet, holding a baby who must be their youngest sister Deborah, the other red-headed and a ball of energy, busy hauling muffins out of the oven.

"Sit down, everyone, while Malena and I get breakfast on the table," Naomi said. "Kate, maybe you could sit across from the twins, next to Adam."

The last place Adam probably wanted her to

sit. But protesting would only add disobedience to her list of sins.

A minute later, there was the sound of boots on the steps, and Kate braced herself. But it was only Zach. Alone.

"He's not in the barn," Zach reported. "Del's still in the home paddock. Looks like he went for a hike."

Delphinium, Kate remembered. The girls had named the cutting horses when they were younger. All after flowers.

"A hike without his breakfast?" Naomi glanced at her husband. "Something is off."

"Maybe he's gone up the mountain," Reuben said. "Like he did when you had little Deborah. Needs some time to himself."

"When he has a guest?" Naomi shook her head, her gaze moving to Kate. "Do you know anything about this?"

Miserably, she nodded.

After a moment, Naomi said, "All right. Let's pray and get some food into us, and then maybe you can explain."

To her silent thanks for the food, Kate added a postscript. *Lieber Vater in Himmel, please let*

Adam be all right. And give me the strength to be truthful.

The sausage and egg casserole flavored with green chiles and dripping with gooey cheese tasted like heaven, as did the blueberry muffins and the potatoes, cut like French fries and baked with olive oil and salt. The generous meal gave her wilting body strength, and when *der Herr* answered her prayer, she just might survive the next half hour.

When she downed the last of her coffee, her hosts seemed to expect her to begin. So she did. Since she was the one at fault, she didn't stint on the details. When it came to Adam's feelings, the thoughts he had written down for Elizabeth's eyes and heart, she chose only the bare minimum. But for the rest? She had no mercy on herself, until she wound up her sorry tale with the buggy ride to the ranch and the news she'd had to break to Adam.

The news it had broken her heart to give.

When she finished, she found that her coffee had been miraculously refilled, and cream added. *"Denki,"* she said in surprise, though she couldn't remember who had done it, and found that trying to hide her burning face behind it didn't do the least bit of good.

"Well, I never," Naomi said at last. "It sounds like a tangle, for sure and certain."

"Not really," Kate said into her cup. "I'll buy a ticket home and Adam will be rid of the Weaver sisters for good."

Malena eyed her. "Are you in love with *mei Bruder*?"

"Malena!" her twin wailed.

"What a question!" Naomi exclaimed. "That is none of your business."

Kate hadn't thought she had any more blushes left, but from the heat in her face, she'd obviously thought wrong. "It's all right," she got out. "He thought he was writing to Elizabeth. I had no right to care. Nothing built on a lie can survive."

"Like a house built on the sand," Reuben agreed. "But don't be too hasty about that return ticket. After this morning, no one from here will be able to take you to the bus station."

"She could call an *Englisch* taxi," Joshua pointed out.

"She could," his father agreed. "But maybe she'd like to join us for turnout on Monday."

"I—I've never ridden a horse," she finally stammered when the shock of surprise had faded a little. "My father is strict about their being used for work, not pleasure."

"Oh, our cutting horses work, you can be sure of that," Reuben said. "My father had the same rule. And when the family first moved here, my mother had a little difficulty with some of the other women riding astride. Said it wasn't modest."

"Until she had no choice," Rebecca put in, making it clear this was a family story, told many times. "They had no hands the first couple of years, so Mammi had to put on a pair of Daadi's denim pants under her dress, borrow some boots from the bishop's wife, and mount up."

"If she hadn't, the starter herd would have cleaned out the home pasture in a month, and starved," Zach explained.

"That's the only time we ever wear pants," Malena chimed in. "For spring turnout, and autumn roundup. Otherwise it's my brothers and the hands who work the cattle on the cutting horses."

"Our neighbors, men and women, all turn out to help at those times of the year," Reuben resumed, "and we help them in our turn. The hands have all hired on, but still. We'd be glad of your help."

It sounded exotic and terrifying to Kate.

Naomi must have seen the expression on her face. "Or you can stay here with me and some of the other women, and help prepare the barbecue in the evening. Sometimes we have as many as forty people here for the meal afterward."

Kate could certainly do that. It was clear from their expressions that the men expected her to. But when would she get another chance to actually live the things that Adam had written about?

The truth was, she wouldn't. Not ever.

That decided her. "Can I learn how to ride a horse between now and Monday?"

"I'll teach you," Zach said.

"I will, too," Malena told her. "Our horses make it easy. They're trained to respond to body language, so once you learn, you and the horse will be able to communicate."

"If you think so." Kate hesitated. "I'd hate to be responsible for injuring one of your animals just because I'm such a—what's that word?"

"Greenhorn." Malena grinned at her. "Don't worry, our *Schwei* Lovina was the same. But she learned quickly, and so will you."

But from what Adam had said in his letters, Lovina had seen her future here in Montana once she and Daniel had been accidentally reunited at roundup the previous autumn. Kate had no such hope. All she had was a desire to help, as though that could do anything toward making up for the disastrous mistake she had made.

The talk turned toward plans for the day, which seemed to involve giving the calves their shots and branding them and putting tags in their ears. Kate could only hope nobody would ask her to help out with *that*.

Rebecca leaned toward her. "Don't worry. The men look after it. All we have to do is feed them when they all come in for *Middaagesse*. With the hands and you, we'll be about fifteen—more if Noah King and his brothers Andrew and Simeon come."

"Noah wouldn't miss an opportunity to see my little *Schweschder*, even if it means he has to learn to brand and tag," Zach teased.

"He plans on having his own ranch someday, so you know he will," Rebecca informed her brother down her nose. "It's not just to see me."

Naomi pushed her chair away from the table. "Rebecca, maybe you can show Kate her room, and then we'll get breakfast cleared up."

Rebecca led the way upstairs, while Kate followed her marveling at the log construction of the house that felt solid and spacious all at once. She was shown into a room that looked out on the bends of the river in the valley. On the bed was a quilt that gave the Mariner's Compass a whole new meaning, done in shades of green from dark hunter to the delicate greenish-yellow of a spring leaf. The background—a blue so deep it was almost midnight—had stars worked into it in cream.

"Oh, my goodness." Kate leaned closer to examine the detail. "Is that the Big Dipper?"

"*Ja*, it is. My twin has designs like this floating in her head constantly. She made this one for Mamm and Dat's twenty-fifth anniversary. It's the constellations we see here in the autumn."

"*Wunderbaar*," Kate breathed. "*Gott* has given her an amazing talent."

"She's been working up the courage to ask Rose Stolzfus if she'll sell her quilts in her shop. I keep telling her Rose will jump at it, but she's shy."

"Malena?" Kate asked in amazement.

Rebecca laughed. "You sound as if you know her."

"I feel as though I do, from—from Adam's letters." The last words came out practically in a whisper.

Rebecca nodded. "It must have been difficult, the ride home in the buggy. Telling him. I think you're brave, to come all the way out here to do it in person. I don't think I could have."

To give herself something to do, Kate picked

up the roller bag that someone had brought up, and moved it over against the wall. She wouldn't unpack, except for toiletries and a change of clothes. There wasn't any point. After Monday, she'd be gone.

"It was the hardest thing I've ever done," she said. "But I had to. It wasn't bravery. Elizabeth wouldn't write, and no man should hear something like that over the phone. So my only choice was to come myself, and tell the truth about what I'd done."

"What do you mean, your sister wouldn't write? Adam hasn't said a thing about her to us, but all of us could see him waiting for the mail to come, and scribbling late at night when he thought no one was awake."

"Zach must have known. Don't they share a room?"

"Zach isn't the kind of person who needs to know other people's business," Rebecca said. "He's very private. Most of the time even I don't know what he's thinking, unless he's teasing me. Adam usually does, though."

"I wish I had a relationship like that with

Elizabeth," came out of Kate's mouth before her brain could prevent it.

"You're not close?"

Kate turned away to admire the view. "I shouldn't have said that. You'll think Elizabeth is horrible, when I'm the one who's horrible. She has her faults, of course, as we all do, but she's the prettiest girl in the township, aside from maybe Malinda Kanagy. And very sweet natured. It's only writing that ever makes her upset. Mark is lucky, even though his prospects make people think she's the lucky one."

"Oh?"

"His father is going to make him a partner in the farm when they're married. That farm is a big success, and he's the eldest son. Elizabeth won't want for a thing, ever."

Rebecca was silent, and belatedly, Kate realized that might have sounded like a criticism of what Adam had to offer. "I'm sorry, I didn't mean—"

"It's all right," Rebecca said. "I know what you meant."

"So you and Noah…?"

Rebecca blushed and didn't seem to notice

the abrupt swerve in topic. "I'm not used to it, you knowing so much about us. But the answer is, *ja,* we're courting. Out in the open, with our families' approval. My brother Joshua and Sara Fischer will marry in the fall. I think they're planning on early October, once the cattle have shipped and the work winds down for the winter. We'll give my parents a chance to take a breath before we talk about anything more. And Little Joe, too—our bishop. You'll meet him on Monday, since it's our off Sunday this week."

"You call your bishop Little Joe?" Kate asked in amazement.

"He's six foot seven."

"Oh." Adam hadn't thought to mention *that* in all his letters. How funny, the things he took for granted that seemed so strange to her. Women riding horses. Bishops with nicknames. What would she learn next?

Because what she wanted to know most of all was where Adam had gone.

———

ADAM HEARD the measured footsteps approaching through the pines. That narrowed the possibilities down—at least it wouldn't be one of his sisters or, heaven forbid, Kate herself. If he were a betting man, he would bet on Zach. Or Dat. The only two people who knew about his refuge up here.

In a moment, his brother emerged into view between the trunks of the pines, walking the deer trail, and lifted a hand in greeting. Adam remained seated on the rock overlooking this wide meadow. This rock was for him like the one Dat always stopped at during roundup and turnout, simply to take in the grandeur of God's creation. To be grateful for their little place in it. "God is good," he'd say, "and northwestern Montana is the proof." Adam agreed with him, though this view was more intimate. Less grand. At one time he had thought it held his future.

Now he wasn't so sure.

"I thought I'd find you here." Zach climbed up on the rock beside Adam and pulled a paper sack out of the pocket of his barn jacket. "I brought you some breakfast."

He'd left in such a turmoil he hadn't even thought about food until a minute ago. He'd just been contemplating how long he could stay up here before he had to go back to the barn and raid the trail packs for a stale, leftover granola bar.

"Thanks." He took a huge bite of the blueberry muffin and then the tortilla filled with breakfast casserole in the other hand.

"Two-fisting it, huh?" Zach nudged him with his shoulder. "I figured you'd be hungry."

"Is everyone mad at me?" he said with his mouth full.

"Why would they be? Mamm says it's a tangle, for sure and certain."

"It is not." He swallowed, then took another enormous bite. "Kate Weaver has been lying to me for more than a year."

"Sounds like her sister might have had a part in it, too."

"Don't you say anything against Elizabeth."

Zach fell silent at the ferocity in Adam's tone.

The silence dragged on for the rest of the

burrito. Adam returned to the muffin, and finished it in three bites. "Sorry."

Zach nodded, accepting his grudging excuse for an apology. "Dat's invited her to stay for turnout."

"What?" Adam turned to him incredulously. "Why?"

"Mostly because everyone is going to be too busy to get her back to Libby, and the train only stops four days a week. What's she going to do, sleep at the bus station all weekend and eat out of the vending machine?"

"Of course not," he grumbled. She could stay at Mountain Home's only motel. But it catered mostly to hunters and fishermen, not lone Amish girls who probably didn't have the money to pay for a room anyway. It would look beyond strange for Mamm to arrange for her to stay with one of the other Amish families, after she'd travelled for three days across the country to reach the Circle M. Of course she had to stay at the ranch.

He didn't, though. "Guess I'll be camping up here, then."

"Dat might have something to say about that. Branding today and tomorrow."

His life might have fallen to pieces, but there were still calves needing to be branded and innoculated and tagged, and what was more important? The family's livelihood or his broken heart?

"At least she'll be in the house," he muttered.

"Probably," Zach agreed easily. "She looked a bit sick at the idea of branding. But Malena and I are going to teach her to ride well enough to come up the mountain. She's never been on a horse, she says."

Adam rolled his eyes to *Himmel*, where *der Herr*—for reasons known only to Him—was *not* answering his fervent prayers. "Easy enough to keep a few hundred head between me and her, I guess."

"She's not so bad, *Bruder*," Zach said. "She told us the whole truth. Admitted her mistake. You're the only one who hasn't forgiven her."

Adam groaned and crossed his arms on his knees, dropping his forehead on them. Great. Now the whole family knew how clueless and stupid he'd been, getting taken in by that girl. He'd been so in love he hadn't even realized the author of Elizabeth's letters had changed in midstream.

"It took courage to do that," his brother went on, looking almost as though he were meditating on the view of the little meadow, with the mountains rising in the distance above the treetops. Sometimes he did that before he got out his pen and paper to draw. "A lot of courage to be honest about what she'd done. And why she'd done it."

"All right, since you're such a fan of hers. Why did she do it?" The answer to that had eluded him from the moment she'd spoken his name at the bus station.

Zach chuckled. "Malena came straight out and asked if she was in love with you."

Adam stopped himself from groaning a second time. "Only Malena. What did Kate say?"

"She didn't really answer. Only said that it was the way you wrote that touched her heart."

"Those words were meant for Elizabeth! It was *her* heart I was trying to touch. Kate had no business even seeing them."

"I'd say you ought to take that up with

Elizabeth, who seems to have been happy to let Kate write for her. And apologize for her." He paused. "Oh, wait. You can't write to a girl who's engaged to someone else, can you? That wouldn't look so *gut*."

Adam might have growled into his forearms. "Don't you have calves to tag?"

"*Ja*. So do you."

"Maybe I should sleep in the bunkhouse."

"You'd rather put up with the *Englisch* hands' video games and snoring than sleep in your own bed?"

He rocked his head back and forth on his arms. "Why didn't she tell me she wanted to break up?" His voice was muffled, but Zach's hearing was acute. "Why lead me on for six more months when she was already dating someone else?"

"Kate might know."

"I'm not talking to Kate."

"Maybe you should. She seems like a good person."

"She's a deceiver."

"Harsh, *Bruder*."

"I feel harsh. I feel like a fool. And it hurts."

He lifted his head. "She's so beautiful, Zach. A face that stops you in your tracks and makes you forget to breathe."

"Hard to get any work done that way," Zach pointed out.

"You know what I mean."

"Nobody has that effect on me, so *neh*, I don't. But there must be more to this Elizabeth than just looks. I know you wouldn't put a greater store in that than all the other qualities a man looks for in a wife. Especially a ranch wife."

"I haven't seen her in two years," Adam admitted. It sounded as though he had been under a prison sentence. "Up until this morning I would have stood in front of the bishop and said that of all the women in the world, I knew her inside and out. But now…" His voice trailed away. He had been set free, and until this morning had not known he had been in captivity. He missed it.

"Now," Zach mused aloud, "I'd say Kate is really the one you know inside and out. Right?"

A shaft of pure anger sent Adam scrambling to his feet. He climbed off the rock and barely managed to keep his feet on the steep stretch of scree between it and the grassy meadow.

"Going somewhere?" Zach called.

"No. Not anymore." He headed for the woods. Putting as many pines between him and the truth as possible.

It took about ten minutes before the tears of rage cleared from his eyes and he realized that he was already on the way home.

Chapter 6

BY LUNCH TIME, Kate had given up trying to catch a glimpse of Adam. In any case, there was no time for gazing out the windows to look for him, because of all weekends for her to arrive unexpectedly, this was one of the busiest of the year for the family on the ranch.

"We have about a hundred calves," Malena explained as they washed and dried the dishes and cleaned up the kitchen after breakfast. "Each one has to be branded and tagged and given their shots. Then, when roundup comes in September, we'll know which of them is ours."

"Aren't they fenced?" she asked Rebecca as they swept the kitchen, living room, both mud rooms, and the bathroom before the entire crew came in from the paddocks for lunch.

"Neh," Rebecca said. "Once we take them past the collection pens at the foot of the mountain, they'll follow their mothers up to the alpine pastures and we won't see them again. No fences up there on BLM land."

Kate could hardly get her mind around it. "In Whinburg Township, every field is fenced so the cows don't get out on the road."

"No roads up there, either," Malena said, polishing the wood surfaces of the furniture. "Just a cut line here and there, and a couple of fire lookouts."

Kate learned what a fire lookout was—a tower where a lone ranger spent days at a time, watching for the telltale plume of a forest fire. She learned what the calves were inoculated for—viruses and bacteria that even Rebecca couldn't pronounce. And by pure chance, she learned what Adam's favorite food was—barbecued ribs done over a slow fire with a homemade hot sauce their aunt in New Mexico sent every year at Christmas. Not that she'd ever get a chance to use any of these bits of learning, especially the last one. But she filed them away all the same. He'd shared so much in his letters, it surprised her that his favorite dish hadn't come up.

But there was no sharing now.

The branding crew of about fifteen men, young and old, walked up the slope to the deck behind the house, where a long table had been set up, and a shorter one laden with lunch—a big pot of stew, spicy chile con carne, several kinds of salad, and more cornbread muffins than Kate had ever seen at one time before, except maybe at a barn raising. Adam sat at the far end of the table, but the bishop, who was seated opposite her, distracted her with conversation and she lost sight of him.

Little Joe Wengerd was the kind of man you couldn't ignore, even if he hadn't been chosen by lot to shepherd the church in the Mountain Home district. His size, for one thing. And his voice, deep and resonant and carrying as any foghorn. His laugh was like that, too. It turned out he was cousin to Lovina Wengerd Lapp

Miller, Daniel's bride of only a couple of weeks.

"Their honeymoon visits will be short—only a couple of weeks," Little Joe told her, shoveling in stew with relish. "Daniel is needed here. First stop in Whinburg Township will likely be Melvin and Carrie Miller. Relatives of the family here on the ranch. You know them?"

"Of course," she told him. "They're in a different district on the far side of Whinburg, while we're closer to Willow Creek, but we know each other pretty well." Well enough for Naomi to have written the news about Adam and Elizabeth to Carrie, who had unwittingly brought disaster down on Kate's head when she'd spoken to Elizabeth that day in town.

Little Joe nodded at her plate. "How do you like the stew? It's Naomi's specialty."

"It's delicious. Different. I can't put my finger on why, though."

"It's elk."

Kate stopped chewing, then swallowed. "No wonder. Funny, I never thought I'd see the day when I ate elk stew."

"Around here, most of the men are hunters.

Not like these *Englisch* hunters you see flying in on their private planes and not allowing anyone else on the allotment. But once the cattle come down in the fall, we don't have far to go to find prime hunting land."

"And the freezers in town are filled for another year?" Adam had written something similar in a letter last year.

"*Ja.*" The bishop washed down his muffin with half a glass of homemade root beer. "In the summer, it's a little harder to get away because there's so much to do, but come a beautiful long afternoon, you can find those river bends down there dotted with fishermen in Amish straw hats, reeling in that evening's dinner." He paused, his gaze rising in the opposite direction, to the mountain behind them. "It's a powerful lot of work, ranching, but I wouldn't trade it for anything. I'm thankful every day that *der Herr* directed me here all those years ago."

"I am, too, Dat." A slender young woman with dark hair and eyes of the same intense blue as Little Joe's settled beside him on the bench and dug into her meal. "Nice as it is back in Whinburg Township, I'd rather live here."

The bishop grinned and tilted the last of it at Kate. "Have you met my youngest *Dochsder?* Ruby, this is Kate Weaver."

"Not yet." Kate offered a shy smile.

"Nice to meet you," Ruby said. "That's my mother, Sadie, over there, in the purple dress, dishing up stew."

So these were the bishop's wife and daughter. "Do you have brothers and sisters in the valley?"

Ruby nodded, as Little Joe got up to cajole seconds from his wife. "Two of each, married and with families. I'm the last one at home." Zach ambled past and gave them a nod before he went to join the rowdy table of young men at the far end of the deck. Ruby watched him go, then tilted her head in that direction. "With Zachariah are the Yoder brothers, wearing the green shirts, and the man in blue without his hat is Simeon King."

"Noah King's brother?"

"You know him?" Ruby looked at her curiously, but Kate shook her head.

"Rebecca mentioned they might come this morning, that's all."

"She would, I suppose. Over there with the crutches is the middle brother, Andrew. He's a bit of a black sheep. Jumped the fence twice. But now it looks like he might be making up his mind. Of course, a broken leg and a dislocated shoulder will slow you down some. Give you time to think." At Kate's questioning glance, she added, "He was in a car accident early last month."

A car accident. Not a buggy accident. Interesting that Adam hadn't mentioned *that* in his last letter. She wondered why.

"How long do you plan to stay?" Ruby asked.

Of course she was making conversation. Surely no one had been talking about what had brought her out here.

"Not long," she hedged. "But I am excited about helping with spring turnout on Monday. Mind you, I have to learn to ride a horse before then, or they'll be pulling me up the mountain in a pony cart."

Ruby smiled at the picture it made. Her whole face changed when she smiled, losing its seriousness and leaving you unable to look away.

"Malena and Zach have said they'll teach me," Kate went on after a moment. "Once the calves are looked after, I expect."

"They should have it done by midday tomorrow," Ruby said. "Maybe I could come over and help with the lessons?"

"I'd love it if it were anything else," Kate assured her, "but the fewer people who see me make a fool of myself, the better."

"You won't. Riding is kind of instinctive."

"That's what Malena says. I'm to communicate with my horse using body language."

"What does Zach say?" Ruby sounded almost hesitant.

"Zach doesn't say much at all." She laughed. "Which from my point of view is probably a good thing."

One of the other *Youngie* called to Ruby and she gave a quick smile to Kate before she took her plate over to join the girl. Kate felt unexpectedly alone in the laughing, talking crowd. Did Ruby know she had this effect on people—making them feel welcome and that they had a friend in a strange place? Her cousin

Grant Weaver's wife, Emma, believed that *Gott* sent little gifts along the way, some to teach a lesson, some simply to make His children happy. It was up to them to notice the generosity of His hand. Kate decided she would take Ruby's quiet, open friendliness for what it was—a little gift.

"Are you finished?" came a voice behind her. "I've just fed Deborah, and burped her. Can you take her for a minute while I get some lunch?"

Kate turned to find Naomi standing there, holding the baby. "I'd love to."

"*Denki*, Kate. I'm so hungry Deborah is lucky I'm not sucking on her dimpled little elbows." With a laugh, Naomi handed her over and hustled away to fill a plate.

"Well, hello, *Liebling*," she said to the child, whom she'd only seen sporadically during the busy morning. "What do you think about all these people, hey?"

The baby was too young to do much but blink and gurgle, having only come into the world at the beginning of April. It suddenly occurred to her to wonder if the baby's birth and the King boy's accident had happened at the same time. Kate supported her head and cuddled her, all wrapped in her blanket though the day wasn't cold. She loved the sensation of holding a baby—their weight, their warmth, even their wiggliness when they weren't comfortable and were trying to let you know.

"You don't mind strangers, little one?" she murmured. "What a *gut Boppli* you are, to let me hold you. You're another little gift, aren't you?"

Big blue eyes gazed up at her. What little hair there was on her head was tinged with red in the sunlight.

Smiling, Kate lifted her head from her contemplation of the baby, to look straight into Adam's eyes. He was standing stock still on the other side of the table, staring at her as if she were a raccoon trying to steal something off a plate. Before she could utter a word, he scowled and walked off, his boot heels thudding on the sturdy planks of the deck.

He might as well have slapped her.

Stricken, Kate took refuge in the baby, cuddling her and murmuring nonsense. "*Dei Bruder* is a cranky one, isn't he, *Liebling*? But he needn't worry. I'll be out of his hair just as soon as I can."

"Whose hair?" Naomi put a loaded plate on the table and slid in beside her. "She give you any trouble?"

Kate chose to answer the second question. "This little bit of sunshine? *Neh,* not at all. She's going to be a redhead, isn't she? We've been getting acquainted and having a lovely time."

"I'm glad someone is having a lovely time. I saw my son give you the stinkeye just now."

Was there nothing this woman missed? Kate was silent while Naomi addressed herself to her lunch. After a minute, the latter said, "Don't be discouraged by Adam. He's had a terrible disappointment. At the moment, he's blaming the messenger."

"As he should," Kate said glumly. "Since the messenger wrote the messages."

"Far be it from me to criticize someone I've never met, but I can't help but feel that the image in his mind that he calls Elizabeth had at least an equal share in the mess. I can't imagine why she didn't simply write to tell him the correspondence was over when she began seeing someone else."

Kate wondered dazedly if this woman was as blunt with everyone, or if she was normally this mother-bear-like on the subject of her cubs.

As if she had read her mind, Naomi chuckled. "Sorry. My *Kinner* say I have no filters. I'm trying to develop them, but it might take my whole life. Sometimes I'm lucky and a straightforward speech clears the air. Sometimes I'm not, and I cause offense. If I've offended you, I apologize."

"You haven't." Kate finally found her tongue, and adjusted the baby's weight in her arms. The tiny, perfect eyelids were fluttering closed. "At the time, I didn't think to wonder. About what you said. But I had a few days on the train to think about it. My sister, she…" How could she put this without sounding jealous? "She's very pretty. She attracts all kinds of attention, and I suppose she's become used to it. So having two boys or more on the string is kind of normal for her."

"Doesn't excuse the correspondence." Naomi savored a forkful of pickled beans.

"I suppose not. But if you knew her, you might understand."

"Do the boys in your district understand?"

Kate had never given it any thought. "I don't know. But the ones who tried to get to her through me got short shrift. She always told me that a man should be up front about courtship, and not come at it sideways."

"Is she older or younger than you?"

"Younger."

Naomi made a sound that might have been disbelief. Or maybe it was the vinegar in the pickles.

"And this Mark Yoder? What is he like?"

"He's nice. Baptized, like she is. He's like the male version of Elizabeth—the girls have been making eyes at him since he was a scholar. The pack fell away one by one because once Elizabeth looked at him, all that was over. I'm pleased for them, truly. Anyone who can tolerate multiple trips to town to decide on wedding invitations has to be not only patient, but kind as well."

"A sign of true love." Naomi smiled in the direction of her husband, who seemed to sense it, and turned from the group of men he was talking with. Unerringly, his gaze found his wife in the crowd. "I remember a man who helped with all the preparations for a wedding, and it wasn't even his." Reuben smiled back at Naomi, and Kate felt a pang in her heart.

What would it be like to still be in love, thirty years on? Would she ever get the chance to find out?

Naomi peered into the blanket at her daughter. "Asleep. That means I can have dessert. Back in a minute."

When she returned, in each hand she carried a slab of blueberry pie with a dollop of whipped cream on top. "Sadie Wengerd makes this. Best ever."

"That's the bishop's wife?"

"*Ja*. One of my dearest friends." Naomi savored the pie.

Kate wondered if the same blissful expression was on her own face. Definitely the best ever.

"Can I give you some advice, Kate?"

She wasn't certain what the topic would be, but she could guess. "I hope you will."

"Be patient with Adam. He's always been a bit of a dreamer. And a dream as cherished as this has been will hurt when it's taken away."

Kate could be blunt, too. "It won't really matter, though, will it? By this time next week, I'll be on a train again, heading east."

"Is that what you want?"

No, it wasn't. Now that she'd done what she'd come out here to do—confessed her sin, given him the news of Elizabeth's engagement—she had to admit to herself that she'd had her own dreams, too. But the last thing she could do was admit them to Adam's mother, out here in public.

Even if the only person within earshot was the baby.

"It doesn't matter what I want," she mumbled around a mouthful of blueberries and flaky short crust. "*Gott* hasn't pointed out the path He wants for me, that's all."

Naomi was thoughtful for a moment, scraping up the last remnants of pie. "Let me ask you this, then. If there were no Elizabeth in the picture, would you stay for a while?"

"*Ach, ja,*" came out of her mouth like a pair of

birds startled off a branch, acting solely on instinct. But Kate couldn't afford to keep blurting things out like this. "The fact is that Elizabeth *is* in the picture. Not in a practical sense, but she is when it comes to Adam's feelings. And a week is not long enough for him to forgive me for what I did."

"Unforgiveness is a sin."

"I'm sure he knows that. But it will be more difficult if I'm here in his face, reminding him of my own sin."

"Is that what caused you to write those letters for Elizabeth? Deliberate sin? For your own amusement, or hers?"

"*Neh*," Kate whispered, shocked to the core that Naomi could think such a thing.

"Then why? Help me understand." She held out her arms for the baby.

Kate had reached the end of her rope. She could never say out loud what lay in her heart. What she'd so foolishly exposed in those letters Adam believed to have come from Elizabeth.

She handed Deborah to Naomi. "Excuse me," she mumbled. "Can I take your plate?" And she picked up their dishes and fled.

Chapter 7

WITH DEBORAH ASLEEP on her shoulder, Naomi Miller slid in next to Sadie Wengerd after the kitchen screen door slammed behind Kate. Her friend frowned at her as she eyed the last piece of the blueberry pie sitting there so defenselessly in the middle of the table.

"Don't you dare," Sadie said. "My *Mann* hasn't had his pie yet and you'll break his heart. Speaking of, what have you been saying to poor Kate Weaver? She looked as though she was about to cry."

"I'm trying to get to the bottom of this."

Naomi did her best to lay out a complicated situation as simply as possible.

"So that's what has brought her here," Sadie breathed. "Now it makes sense. What a brave young woman, to want to confess in person. Not take the easy way out."

"My thoughts exactly. But she can only see the sin, not the confession of it."

"So the truth has not set her free."

"Not yet." Naomi lifted her eyes unto the hills standing guard over the Circle M and the Siksika Valley. *From whence cometh my help.* "I tried to ask her why she had done it—written those letters from her heart and then signed her sister's name to them. I can only think of one reason."

"So can I." Sadie's gaze met hers.

Naomi whispered, "*Die Maedel* is in love with my boy."

"I think it must be so. Who else would care so much about a man's feelings but the woman who has feelings for him?"

It was not nearly the first time that Sadie and she had been of one mind on a given subject. Perhaps it was their friendship as

Youngie, and bringing up families together in the same church district. Or perhaps it was because they both had the gift of discernment, which in Sadie's case had stood her in good stead ever since the day Little Joe had opened the *Ausbund* and found the long piece of hay inside. A bishop's wife had nearly as much to do in the shepherding of the flock as her husband.

"What do you think she'll do?" Sadie asked, filching a chocolate chip cookie off a nearby plate.

"She thinks she's staying for turnout, then going home as soon as she can book a seat on the train."

"Something tells me you don't agree."

"She did a foolish thing, I'll admit. And it has hurt my son. That part is between the two of them."

"But?"

"But surely there must be a way to help it along. Because for sure and certain forgiveness will not be given and accepted within the next week. I know my Adam."

"He finds it hard to forgive?"

Naomi shook her head. "He finds it hard to

let go of dreams. And Elizabeth was the biggest, brightest dream of all, if I'm not mistaken. Apparently she is very lovely. He has invested her earthly vessel with Kate's personality and spirit, and is in love with a perfect woman. It's a pity she's only a figment of his imagination."

"I was like that, once." Smiling, Sadie leaned her chin on one hand. "Such a crush I had on Jeb Kuepfer, my goodness me. Remember him?"

"Has he ever come back to church?"

Sadie straightened, her eyes sad for the lost sheep. "Not that I've ever heard. So you've told me what Kate is planning to do. But what does *mei Freinde* Naomi Miller plan to do?"

Naomi smiled the kind of smile that never failed to raise a look of alarm on Reuben's face.

"Well, I can't very well confiscate the ranch phone or the fire phone to keep her from calling Amtrak. But I can make sure both Reuben and Adam carry them with them out in the paddocks. I can also make it nearly impossible to find a horse or a buggy available to get to the bus station. Which is where I'll need your help. Yours is the closest place to find a ride if one is not to be found here."

"You're such a brat," Sadie told her affectionately. "What will you do if she simply decides to pack up her things and walk the five miles into town?"

"I'll jump off that bridge when I come to it," Naomi said.

The men seemed to recollect all at the same time that work needed to be done this afternoon, and the deck emptied as they walked down to the paddocks in twos and threes. Adam, of course, had gone long before. She could see him out in the calves' paddock on Del, cutting the first animals out of the bawling herd and guiding them into the squeeze for their shots. Zachariah, never one to let a man work alone, particularly his brother, had mounted up on Rosie and was already riding out to assist.

Work could be an antidote to a hurting heart —she knew that as well as anyone. But maybe work was not the right solution here.

Maybe love was the only cure. And not the kind of love that could be satisfied with longing and distance and imagination, but the kind based in common experience, and appreciation, and friendship.

She would have a little word with Reuben in the privacy of their room tonight. And once he got done hooting with laughter at her and her ideas, she just might try her hand at some good old-fashioned matchmaking.

After all, half the work was already done for her.

ADAM HAD LEARNED as a small boy that there were aspects of ranching that had to be endured, since they couldn't be enjoyed. Things that were done for the safety of the animals. He wasn't the only one in his family who looked at inoculating, tagging, and branding the calves as a necessary price to pay in order to get to the other side, which was turning the animals loose in the summer pastures. The calves would soon forget the stress of today in the prospect of grass and freedom over several months' worth of tomorrows.

In his mind, Kate was another thing that had to be endured, not enjoyed. Luckily, he had enough to do that they didn't need to be within a hundred yards of each other right up until the day she left. He'd stand politely with his family and wave her off down the lane, heave a sigh of relief, and have the rest of his life to figure out how he was going to live with the giant hole in his heart shaped like Elizabeth.

For about the hundredth time, misery slashed through him in a cold wave. He swung his lasso and missed the calf hightailing it for the fence, and had to bring Del around with his knees to try again. Zach rode in front of him, his loop settling neatly over the calf's head as though guided by an unseen hand. Rosie sat back on her haunches and the runaway came to a halt in a cloud of dust, bawling at the unfairness of life.

"Something on your mind?" Daniel hollered from the squeeze, grinning as Zach guided the runaway over.

Adam made a sound in his throat that was half groan, half growl. He should talk—it wasn't so long ago that Lovina had put Daniel's heart through its paces, too. You'd think he'd have a little more sympathy.

But if Adam didn't get his mind back on his

work, Dat would notice. For the rest of Friday afternoon, there was plenty of work to keep a man's mind busy. Working with the cutting horses came so naturally to him it wasn't often he took a moment to realize it made him happy. The feeling crept up on him, as though *der Herr* was reminding him that there were still good things in the world, even if the biggest thing was now only a beautiful, forbidden memory.

How had his bright future become only a memory so quickly?

He shook the thought away and headed off another calf at the pass.

They worked until sunset, his brothers and the hired hands becoming more of a team with each passing hour. Dat had expected they would be finished the following day, and as usual, he turned out to be right. Around lunchtime on Saturday, they got the last of the calves back to their mothers in the biggest paddock, ready to begin their long walk on Monday.

Adam gave Del an extra helping of oats to thank him for a job well done, and rubbed him down before turning him out into the home pasture with the other cutting horses. After showers and fresh pants and a shirt, he joined everyone at the big kitchen table for the midday meal. Kate didn't look up as he took a seat as far from her as he could. Nor did he attempt conversation. He was as hungry as a bear despite the big breakfast he'd eaten at five a.m., and the pans of enchiladas and the chicken taco stew disappeared quickly once the crew got started.

Dat asked him for more details about the state of the gates and fences on the way to the allotment, and his reply was the only time he spoke.

He spent the next couple of hours with his brothers, cleaning tack and getting their equipment ready, since church was tomorrow and no work could be done. The trail packs were checked and brought up to the house, ready to be filled with food. They made sure the horses had received no injuries or picked up any stones during the busy past couple of days, and would be healthy for Monday's strenuous ride.

As he came out of the barn, he looked up just in time to see Malena lead Marigold, tacked up a second time, out into the corral, followed by Kate Weaver in boots and jeans under a taupe dress. Her hair was bound up in a *Duchly*, and Malena snugged her own raggedy hat down on her head.

Was she really going to do this? Learn to ride today?

"Poor Marigold," he said to Zach, who was right behind him. He hooked a thumb in the direction of the corral. "Doesn't seem fair to make her work again."

"Poor Kate," Zach replied, ambling over to rest a boot on the lower rail of the fence and fold his arms on the upper.

Aw, he wasn't going to be the audience, was he? Adam should just go get the mail—

Neh. There was nothing in the mail for him. Not now.

Still, anything was better than watching a greenhorn wear a horse out when she should just stay in the kitchen with Mamm on Monday. It would be more work than it was worth to keep an eye on her so she didn't fall off or get hurt by a runaway animal. Any happiness he might have felt this morning with the horses leached away like rain into parched earth, while his long-legged stride took him swiftly up the pine-shaded lane a quarter mile to the mailbox.

And there it was—the familiar envelope with a funny sticker on the flap, the handwriting that never failed to make his heart jump in his chest.

Except it wasn't Elizabeth's handwriting. He knew now it was Kate's. He should just throw it away.

Did you get my—her—last letter? The words she'd said to him when he'd collected her on Thursday echoed in his memory. With a sinking in his gut, he realized this must be it, two days late. He tucked the rest of the mail under his arm and ripped open the envelope.

The familiarity of that neat, orderly handwriting, the spirit that lay in the words, the affection—

He groaned and lifted his head, his gaze seeking out the snowy heights of the mountains. When he had himself under control, he scanned through the closely written paragraphs, filled with descriptive turns of phrase and humor. He'd come to love getting a letter with the Whinburg postmark. Now it made him feel sick.

And then … there it was.

> I've become good friends with a young man here called Mark Yoder. I think you might have met him when you were here that summer. He's been taking me home from singing and my parents have made him welcome here at the farm. I hope you will forgive me. There must be a dozen girls in Montana who would jump at the chance for a ride home from singing with you, Adam. I don't mean to hurt you, and I hope you will understand. Sometimes our hearts change with the seasons of life, the way the leaves on the trees change.
>
> I wish you every blessing God has in store for you.

"Good friends?" he demanded aloud. "Good friends—when you were already engaged to him? How can you write such a lie and look me in the face?"

Two crows cawed at him, as though imitating his raised voice.

He glared at them. "Shut up!"

Had Elizabeth told Kate to write those words? Or had Kate come up with the lie all by herself? He was half tempted to march back to the paddock, shake the letter in her face, and demand an answer. No wonder she'd asked him if he'd received it. It would have greased the skids for the news she'd been about to ruin his life with on the way home. But at least then he could have caught her out in the lie.

He crumpled the letter into a ball and walked back to the house, fuming.

If only it wasn't Sunday tomorrow—and turnout the day after. If all this had happened last week, he could have gone camping in his secret spot and found some kind of peace. But now all he could do was turn his back on the riding lesson in the corral, take the mail in, and find a measure of refuge for an hour up the hill in Mammi's orchard.

He got through dinner somehow, listening with half an ear to Malena regaling everyone with how well Kate had done on horseback.

Why couldn't she have been so afraid of horses she would have admitted her place was in the home? But no. She and Marigold had taken to each other, to the point that Dat assigned that horse to her for Monday. "She's older and experienced," he said to Kate, whose face had lit up with delight. "Just let her work, and try to stay on."

Adam burned with resentment that she could look so happy when he was so miserable. Once dinner was over and the dishes had been done, there was still no escape. Because it was Saturday night, and they would read the Scriptures together, round robin fashion.

"Tomorrow's sermon is on faith," Dat said, "so we'll prepare ourselves and think on our own faith. The substance of things hoped for. The evidence of things not seen."

Elizabeth. The substance of things hoped for.

And Kate. The evidence of things not seen. For only *Gott* had seen the deception going on behind that quiet face, those downcast eyes.

"These all died in faith, not having
received the promises, but having
seen them afar off, and were persuaded of
them, and embraced them,
and confessed that they were
strangers and pilgrims on the earth."

Adam's gaze moved from one of his family to the next. When the old Bible reached Kate, he couldn't watch as she read. He couldn't very well put his hands over his ears, so he had to listen to that soft voice. The kind of voice that found the music in words thousands of years old.

"But now they desire a better country, that is, an heavenly; wherefore God is not ashamed to be called their God: for he hath prepared for them a city."

She handed the Bible to Malena, but Adam's hard-earned internal quiet was broken. It was all he could do to settle his mind enough to pray after Dat read the last verses, bowing his head for the silent communion with *Gott*.

Vater in Himmel, please help me through the days until she leaves the ranch. I'm trying not to harbor a spirit of unforgiveness, but the burden is too big for me. Help me, Lord, to set it aside by keeping her out of sight. I ask this in Your Son's name. Amen.

Afterward, everyone stirred and Sara and Rebecca took the babies away to put them to bed. The sun was still a glow in the sky—what Mamm called the "gloaming." As though he'd summoned her, his mother touched his arm.

"*Mei Sohn*, before we go to service tomorrow, I think it would be wise if you had a talk with Kate."

He blinked at her, horrified, while his delicious supper turned over like a capsizing rowboat in his stomach. The *gut Gott* sure had a strange way of responding to prayers.

"I know your feelings are getting the better of you," she went on softly, "but don't you think it would be wise to have things settled before we meet with *Gott*?"

"There's nothing to settle," he croaked. "I have nothing to say."

"Maybe she does."

"She's already said far more than anybody should. In writing."

"Adam." Mamm gazed at him. "Let not the

sun go down upon your wrath. You've allowed it once. Don't allow it tonight as well. Not before church."

His parents had made another vow on their wedding day. A vow between themselves alone. *Let not the sun go down upon your wrath.* That meant to make up a quarrel before you sleep, or like a silent, unwelcome third party, it would still be there the next day, and follow both of you wherever you went, becoming more and more intractable as the day wore on.

They'd taught all their children the same, sometimes by example, sometimes in words of encouragement. Just like this.

He sighed. "All right."

"Take her for a walk down by the river. She might enjoy the light on the water."

He nodded, and prepared himself to obey.

But was it true obedience when your body did as it was asked, but your spirit howled its unwillingness all the way?

Chapter 8

IN THE DREAM world that Kate occasionally inhabited when she was half asleep in bed, or doing a chore that didn't require concentration, she walked on the bank of a river hand in hand with Adam Miller. Sometimes it was sunset, the light soft and romantic, bringing out the red highlights in his brown hair as he leaned in for a kiss. Sometimes it was simply a walk to enjoy the beauty of the day. Sometimes there was even snow, with blue shadows in the drifts and snowflakes on their eyelashes.

She'd never dreamed anything like this.

He'd asked her to come for a walk the way a

policeman asked for your identification card after stopping the buggy. He led the way down to the river on a well-worn path, not looking back to see if she was keeping up. When he finally stopped, it was on a gravel bar formed by a deep bend, the water rushing as it ran over the stones.

"The current looks slow from the house," she ventured, pushing through the last of the willows and joining him. "But it's not."

"Spring runoff."

"Still? In the middle of May?"

"We had snow two weeks ago. And breakup was only last month."

"What's that?" He couldn't mean Elizabeth. That wouldn't make sense.

"When the ice thaws and breaks up. The river is always moving underneath, but the ice was thick this year. Took a while. We had a lot of freezes and snows last winter."

This was the most he'd said to her in two days. No wonder people talked about the weather when they couldn't think of anything else to say.

"Do you skate on it when it's like that?

Frozen thick? We do. Not on the creek. You can't trust it. But the ponds."

He nodded, hands on hips, looking at the opposite bank. Glaring at it, really. "We make one hockey team. The Yoders and some of the other *Youngie* make another."

"Who plays goal?"

His gaze lifted to the new house in the distance, on the edge of the water meadows, its windows facing them. "My brother Daniel. I guess now he can teach Joel how to be backup goalie."

"Joel—Lovina's boy. We went to church with them in Whinburg Township." She dared to smile, though he wasn't looking at her. "What a shock to everyone when her first husband was killed. I'll be happy to see her tomorrow. Where is church?"

"The bishop's. We'll all probably walk. Dat will take Mamm and Sara with the babies in the buggy."

He walked over to the water to look at something and that seemed to be the end of that.

After a minute, she gathered her courage and tried again. "Do you use flies or lures here?"

He glanced back at her, and she felt a tingle of triumph that she'd surprised him. "Flies. Dry. Zach and I tie them to sell at Yoder's Variety Store."

She nodded. "Maybe I could buy a license and wet one or two before I go."

"You fish?" He might have used the same tone to say, *You pet skunks?*

"My father loves fishing almost as much as his Lord, my mother says. He taught me. What flies do you use? Bucktail caddis?"

Again that surprised glance, though it shouldn't have been. She'd seen the caddis hatch yesterday. "Close. Elk hair caddises."

Of course. "Are you a hunter?"

"We all are. Well, not my sisters. Zach and I save as much hair as we can in the fall, to make flies during the winter. When the browns are biting, the tourists will buy a dozen at a time, at six bucks apiece."

"That's what you have here? Browns?"

"And cutthroat, and rainbows."

"What's the limit?"

"Twenty, in possession."

The light glimmered on the water, turning it a kind of gilded silver. As she watched, a trout nosed the surface and gulped a mayfly, making circles ripple outward. "How blessed you are, to live here, and be able to walk down from your house to catch dinner."

"Mamm says that a lot. The twins know a dozen ways to cook trout. I only know one."

"In a pan, fried over a fire?" He was silent, as though waiting for an explanation for her guess. "I got to go on a fishing trip in western Pennsylvania one summer with Dat and my brother and *mei Onkel* who lives out there. I think I was twelve. I can still remember how happy I was to catch the first regulation fish. And how *gut* it tasted."

"Your sister didn't go?"

"Lizzie doesn't like camping," she said before she thought.

"Why not?"

She had no choice but to finish what she'd started, now that she had his complete attention. "Or fish. Or gutting fish. Or mosquitoes. Not that I like those, either, but … she doesn't like things that are messy."

A chill seemed to settle in the air, as though the wind had brushed a glacier on the way down into the valley. Kate wished she hadn't mentioned Elizabeth. But then, how could he not be interested? He had hoped to make her his wife.

"You never mentioned that in her letters," he said.

Kate winced at the pronouns. "It … didn't come up, I guess."

"But you could say things like, *I want to reach all the way to Montana, and talk in person.* Personal things. How could you do that?" His voice carried a raw edge of pain that hurt her heart.

"I meant them," Kate said in a voice so low she hoped he wouldn't catch it, under the sound of the water.

"But I wasn't writing to you."

Her gaze was weighted to the round stones at her feet. "And that was my sin. Please forgive me, Adam." How many times had she begged his forgiveness? Not enough, clearly. "I let my feelings get the better of my sense."

"What feelings?"

He stood there like a tall, accusatory exclamation point.

"I—I had feelings for you. For the man who wrote those letters."

"Elizabeth's man!"

Had any conversation ever been this difficult? But she had to explain. Somehow.

"Not the man who was talking to Elizabeth. The man who loved his home and his God. Who thought things through and talked them over. Who described his family and his life so well I could see it in my head." She gestured outward —at the river, the valley, the Miller homes built by Miller hands. "This place feels as familiar as my own home, because of your letters."

"I hoped it would be Elizabeth's home."

Again that slash of pain through her, deep as the pain in his voice.

She must say something to alleviate that pain or she would weep. "Did you … plan to build here?"

He lifted his head to gaze across the river meadows in the direction of Siksika Lake. "I did."

How sad and full of grief the past tense was!

After a moment, he went on, "My brothers and I are partners in the business, and Dat wants us to. Except Joshua. He's happier with tack and saddles. When he and Sara are married, he'll be moving to her family's hay farm a couple of miles from here. Opening his own shop. He's been apprenticing with a saddle maker to prepare."

"And Rebecca?"

"Noah is a carpenter. If they ever get around to tying the knot, I expect he and his brothers will build a house on the Gingerich place."

"Annie Gingerich?"

Another nod. "She's leaving the farm to his mother. Annie is her *Aendi*."

"No more emergency call-outs?"

"How did you—oh. My letter. *Neh*, no kitchen fires since, and Annie is healing well." He looked up, and frowned. "It feels weird, talking with you about stuff I wrote to her. Did she even read my letters?"

"Sometimes."

He turned away to the river again, probably so she couldn't see his face. After a moment, he cleared his throat. "We should probably go back. It's nearly dark."

"You've probably found your way home from here a hundred times in the dark."

"But you haven't."

Neh. She hadn't found her way home. She may have desired a better country, but the way things were going, it didn't seem as though the *gut Gott* agreed that she should stay.

THERE. He had done his part. Obeyed his mother, heard Kate's apology—again—and now he could approach *der Herr* in church with a clean heart and conscience.

Why, then, weren't his heart and conscience going along with the program?

Adam stood outside the bishop's house with the other young men, all of them dressed in their best black broadfall pants, white shirts, and black waistcoats and hats, the last to go in for church. His heart still felt like a bag of stones, and his conscience was smarting as though every one of those stones had been thrown at it.

"So who's the new girl?" Andrew King seemed to have recovered from Rebecca's refusal to let him court her a couple of weeks ago, and her choosing his brother instead. He leaned on one crutch with one arm and elbowed him in the ribs with the other. "She's staying at the Circle M, ain't so?"

"*Ja*. Going back to Whinburg Township this week sometime."

The Yoder boys had joined them now, sensing gossip the way a range horse senses water. "I heard she was visiting *you*, Miller," David Yoder said.

He shook his head in the negative.

"I heard you've been writing to her sister," Calvin Yoder said. "What I can't figure out is why she's here and not *die Schweschder*."

Adam shrugged, hoping to convey that he didn't care one way or the other. "Looks like we better go in."

"Are you an old lady?" Andrew teased. "Come on. Spill the beans about this girl."

"Her name is Kate Weaver," he said shortly.

"I already knew that. You just don't want to talk about her." Calvin, always the comic, never knew when to leave well enough alone. "That must mean something, hey?"

Adam couldn't say yes. And if he said no, they'd never let up. So he did the only thing he could. He ambled up the kitchen steps, his goal the bench inside where his brother Joshua was already sitting at the back of the congregation, little Nathan in his lap. A man doing child care in church might have shocked some of the old-timers in the congregation, but it seemed perfectly normal to Adam. Joshua and Sara divided parenting between themselves, and his youngest brother never shirked even the messiest of tasks. It was as though he was making up for the *Englisch* mother who had abandoned Nathan at their door, never to be seen again.

Before Adam could get himself safely through the bishop's back door, David Yoder put in the last word. "So she's available, *nix*?"

He would not turn around. He would not react in any way. He even hung onto the door so it wouldn't slam behind him.

In a few minutes, the other guys had filed in as well, Zach had taken his usual seat on his left, and he could only be thankful that in church, at least, he'd be safe from all their talk. They were worse than turkeys in the autumn, gobbling in alarm if a leaf fell or a squirrel ran up a tree.

It was a relief when the *Vorsinger* began the first hymn, but it wasn't until they got to the *Loblied,* and the bishop and ministers came in, that he at last felt safe from the whispers and nudges of his friends. Drat Kate anyway. If she hadn't been sitting up there with his sisters in her heart-shaped Lancaster County *Kapp* and black cape and apron that differentiated her from all the other women, who wore capes and aprons in the same colors as their dresses, he wouldn't be in this uncomfortable situation.

Closing his eyes for prayer, thereby shutting out the sight of her, was an additional relief.

If she had been Elizabeth, he wouldn't have been able to close his eyes, or take them off her for a moment. He would have been the envy of every bachelor in the *Gmay*—even the ones over forty. And his heart would have been light and so full of love that it could have floated out of his body and into her hand, there to stay for the rest of their lives. He was barely aware of singing the next hymn, so vivid were the pictures in his imagination.

"Faith is the substance of things hoped for." Little Joe began his sermon, his booming voice carrying to the very back of the house.

Adam had hoped for so much. Had a faith in Elizabeth that he believed would carry them through a long-distance relationship all the way to a wedding. And it had all been for nothing. Nearly two years of faithfulness—writing every other week, keeping himself from getting too friendly with the other *Maedels* in the valley, working hard to save the money to build a home. He had been happy in his faithfulness. Never grudged a minute of it.

And now?

Well, he supposed he had a healthier bank account than in previous years. But he couldn't kiss that, could he? Or hold it in his arms.

A sudden image flashed into his mind. What

if Elizabeth had used that train ticket and come out to tell him her news himself? What if it had been them in the buggy, on the way home from the bus station? She would have confessed that she had let Kate answer his letters—and sometimes read neither letter nor reply. She would have told him then about Mark Yoder. How would he have felt to get the news from her directly?

He knew how he felt now. Sick at heart. The truth was that no matter which sister had told him about Mark Yoder and his wonderful prospects, the end result would still be the same. Both sisters had sinned. Both had allowed a deception.

But only one had asked his forgiveness for it.

"These all died in faith," boomed the bishop, "not having received the promises, but having seen them afar off."

That's what Kate's letters were. The evidence of things he hadn't seen.

But what was her apology, then? Also evidence of things not seen. *I had feelings for you. For the man who wrote those letters*, she'd said last night. But he didn't want her feelings. His own heart was too bruised to acknowledge them, much less return them.

What he could acknowledge was the bravery it took to tell him about them out loud. On top of coming all this way to tell him what Elizabeth couldn't say—or didn't care enough to say in person.

He could give Kate Weaver nothing.

Nothing except forgiveness. And he hadn't. Not yet.

As his parents had said many a time when he was growing up, faith without works was dead. *Der Herr* had spoken to his heart. He knew now what he had to do.

Chapter 9

KATE HAD ASSUMED that the fellowship meal after church on Sunday would be similar in any Amish community, no matter where you were. From Prince Edward Island to Montana, there would be marshmallow and peanut butter whip for the *Kinner*, and sandwiches and maybe *Bohnesuppe* for the adults. Lots of pickles, and even more pie. After the tables had been set with the tableware and dishes from the bench wagon, she saw all the familiar favorites.

But added to what she expected was the unexpected. Macaroni and cheese in a sauce so creamy it went down like silk. Pickles, yes, but made of every vegetable you could imagine—except watermelon. They didn't grow in Montana. And the sandwiches! They were made of cold elk roast, sliced so thin you could practically see through them, and slathered with homemade horseradish and slices of the cheese that, she learned, the two bachelor Zook brothers made on their farm and sold to a growing clientele of both *Englisch* and Amish through Yoder's Variety Store. She learned double quick that with *this* horseradish, you breathed in through your nose and out through your mouth until the burn dissipated. And then you helped yourself to more.

Kate and the Miller twins helped Ruby Wengerd wash the mountain of dishes afterward, and Adam and Zach helped the bishop's youngest married son load the bench wagon, which would go to his home for the next church Sunday, where the whole process would begin again.

After cleanup was finished, the girls were free to go out into the spring sunshine to visit with the other *Youngie*.

"You'll stay for supper and singing?" Ruby

asked, looking among the three girls from the Circle M. "We won't be late, since most of us will be up at four for turnout."

Malena answered at once. "I expect we all will—maybe even Josh and Sara, too. The good thing is, the walk home isn't far."

Ruby smiled at someone over Rebecca's shoulder. "I expect at least some of the Kings will stay, then."

"For supper and singing?" Noah King joined Rebecca, and Kate, who had been standing next to her, widened their little circle to admit him. "*Ja*, I'll stay. Andrew will too. Don't know about Simeon. He's been spending an awful lot of time at the Bitterroot Dutch Café. I hear tell it's the doughnuts."

Kate had no idea what this meant, other than the news seemed to have electrified both the Miller twins into silence. Even Malena.

"You're joking," Ruby Wengerd finally managed.

Noah shrugged and shifted so his boot heels didn't sink in the soft ground. "The thing about doughnuts is that some people like them, and some people don't. It's all a matter of taste."

"*Neh, neh.*" Malena recovered her powers of speech, waving her hands in front of her face as though she were batting away a wasp. "There must be a new waitress. It isn't—no way—it can't be—"

"Susan?" Ruby's eyes were huge.

"That didn't take long," Rebecca observed.

Malena turned to Kate. "Have you met Susan Bontrager? She chased our brother Daniel for months. She might have run him to ground, too, if it hadn't been for Lovina coming back into his life."

"He would never have been happy with Susan," Rebecca added. "She's far too bossy."

"Not for Sim, it seems," Noah said easily. "He says she's organized. Seems he likes that in a woman."

"Organized is not what I would call it," Malena retorted.

"Does this mean your brothers might stay in the valley?" Rebecca asked Noah.

"Why, would you miss me?" a teasing male voice asked before Noah could do much more than smile and open his mouth.

Kate turned to see Andrew King, his

crutches sinking a little in the grass, as he joined them. "What are you all looking so surprised about?"

"The doughnuts at the Bitterroot Dutch Café," Noah said.

"Ah, the doughnuts. I hear they're an acquired taste."

"Only by some, apparently," Rebecca said, still looking a little dazed. "I may as well ask you, then, Andrew—with this new addition to your brother's diet, do you think you'll all be sticking around?"

Andrew shrugged. "You know diets. They come and go. What I do know is that we're already late heading back, so it's likely we'll be on a train this week, heading east ourselves."

"Ach, neh!" Rebecca clutched Noah's arm. "All of you?"

"We've signed contracts," he told her gently, as if reminding her of something she already knew. "We have to go back and complete the work we promised to do. I don't know about my brothers, but I plan to be back permanently by August. We're still working on the renovations to the farmhouse. I know Sim wants those done before the snow flies."

Which sometimes happened in September, Kate remembered.

"I know you have to go," Rebecca said sadly. "I just didn't realize it would be this week. We'd better enjoy our time together today and tomorrow, hadn't we? Kate is going back this week, too."

"You should book the same train!" Malena exclaimed. "Then at least Kate would have company until Denver."

With a nod, Noah said, "That makes *gut* sense."

"Sense." Andrew snorted, then let his gaze rest on Kate. "It would be *wunderbaar*. I bet Kate appreciates beautiful scenery, too, don't you?"

She had the uncomfortable feeling that she was the beautiful scenery and he was the one appreciating it. If that didn't beat all—she'd seen him twice in her life and already he was flirting!

As if he hadn't noticed her lack of enthusiasm, he lifted his chin in greeting to a newcomer to the circle. "What do you think, Adam? Since we're going back to Amity in a few days and Kate's heading east, too, we should all travel together, *nix*?"

"Who's we?" Adam joined the circle on the other side of Malena, about as far away from Kate as he could be.

"You know as well as your sister that my brothers and I have business to finish in Amity," Noah told him. "But I'll be back as often as I can, courtesy of good old Greyhound."

"I think it's a *gut* idea," Kate ventured. "I wasn't looking forward to that long trip alone. Even if I only have company until Denver, it will be a gift. I was pretty lonesome coming out, and then having to stay awake in the train station in Libby so I didn't miss the first bus to Mountain Home ... well, if I don't have to do that again I'll be happy."

"You didn't sleep in a motel?" Adam frowned.

She shook her head. "The train didn't get in until midnight, and the bus left at five. I didn't think it would be worth spending the money when I probably wouldn't have been able to sleep much anyway."

"Malena could," Rebecca said with a grin.

"You could put her in a luggage rack and she wouldn't know the difference."

"Ha ha," her twin said, making a face at her.

What Kate would never confess was that the journey out here had been one long bad dream. The closer she got to her destination in Montana, the more agitated she'd become over the best way to break her terrible news to Adam. Renting a motel room only to lie there staring at the ceiling and fretting seemed a waste of her slender funds.

"I've got an even better idea," Andrew said. "If you don't have an urgent reason to be back in Whinburg Township, you might get off at Denver and come to Amity with us. You'd be welcome at our cousin Joshua's home. His wife Amanda—"

"Amanda Yoder?" Kate exclaimed. "My goodness, that's right. We saw them on their honeymoon visit. I've known Amanda all my life."

"There you go, then." Andrew looked as smug as though he would be putting her up for an indefinite stay all on his own. "Settled."

"It is *not* settled," Adam said. "Good grief,

Andrew, give the girl a chance to make up her own mind."

"I just did," he said, surprised at Adam's tone.

"It's an option," Kate said hastily. "But one I don't know if I can accept. My mother and sister can only do my share of the work for so long before it becomes more of a burden than a favor."

"They'll have less work with fewer people in the house," Andrew said cheerfully.

"Ask us how we know," Simeon said, strolling up after clearly having heard half the conversation. Hopefully not the part about the doughnuts.

"Baching it is different than managing a house and the garden and helping with the farm," Rebecca said. "I can see Kate's point. I just wish you didn't have to go so soon," she said to Kate. "You only just got here."

How sweet she was. Kate smiled at her in appreciation. At least there was one person on the Circle M who might miss her when she was gone.

She pointedly did not look at the one who wouldn't.

The conversation circles broke up and reformed again and again as the *Youngie* caught up with each other, exchanging news and making plans for the next day. Around three o'clock, Reuben and Naomi left with little Deborah and baby Nathan so that Joshua and Sara could enjoy supper and the singing with their friends. If their wedding was planned around the same time as Elizabeth and Mark's, they wouldn't have so many opportunities left to socialize. The summer would speed by. And after they were married, they wouldn't run with the *Youngie* anymore, but with the other young married couples in the district.

Letting the conversation go on without her for a moment, Kate folded her arms on the top rail of the fence nearby and followed the course of the winding creek, across the valley to the mountains, taking in the beauty of the day. Not that the two groups didn't mix and mingle after church, she supposed, same as in any other district. But her brother's wife had once told her it was a natural progression. The things that interested newlyweds or young couples setting up housekeeping were different from the things that consumed single folks. Like courtship—that had come to its natural conclusion, and had changed its focus to partnership. What a couple considered fun was not what a single thought was fun. For them, *Rumspringe* and making up their minds which side of the fence they were going to live on was a decision made long ago.

"You're looking very thoughtful." David Yoder smiled as he joined her at the fence. He followed the direction of her gaze. "It never gets old, ain't so?"

She quoted softly from one of her favorite Psalms.

> "They go up by the mountains, they go down by the valleys unto the place which thou has founded for them."

"My father quotes that one," David said with a grin. "Usually at roundup, at the top of his lungs, when he's trying to chase calves out of coulees."

She had to laugh at the picture. "What's a coulee?"

"A ravine. Sometimes a dry creek bed.

Always tricky. But if you've got a good horse who knows the land, most times you'll come out all right."

"So you and your brother have hired on at the Circle M for the summer?" When he nodded, she asked, "Doesn't that leave your family two men short?"

"I have more brothers than any man needs," he said. "Dat was glad to get me and Cal off his hands and earning a wage, and Reuben was glad to have us. But everyone pitches in for the big days, like branding and turnout and roundup."

"I even know what all those are, and I've only been here since Thursday," she joked. "I guess it's different with dairy cattle. They come to the milking pen by themselves, don't they?"

"Most of the time. I wouldn't leave them alone altogether, though. One of the family is usually at the gate to remind the stragglers they have work to do. Don't you have dairy cows at all?"

"A few on each place, I guess. The Zook brothers have more, for the cheese. And goats as well." He folded his arms on the top rail, too, and gave her the lightest bump on the elbow with his own. "But I didn't come over to talk about stock. I figured I'd try my luck before you got stuck going home tonight with Andrew King."

Goodness. The young men in Montana didn't beat around the bush. Nobody in Whinburg Township would be this forward after two meetings. "Would that be so bad?"

"Not for him." When he saw her raised eyebrows and dubious expression, he went on, "Nothing against Andrew. But he's a bit wild."

"In what way?"

"He's jumped the fence twice. Says he's come back to the fold for good, but I suppose that's between him and God and his brothers."

"So then …?"

David shrugged. "If you were my sister, I'd say the same things. Just thought you'd like to know. I mean, three weeks ago he was courting Rebecca Miller. More than that—he thought he was engaged to her."

"He *thought* he was?" Rebecca hadn't breathed a word.

"Long story involving a car accident and amnesia. Adam tells it better than me."

In that case, she'd have to live without knowing the details.

"So, can I give you a ride home tonight after singing?"

After a sidelong glance confirmed he was serious, and actually looked gratifyingly nervous about her reply, she said, "You know it's only across the highway and down a bit, *nix*?"

He grinned and seemed to take encouragement. "I figure we either leave before the Millers do, or after they're gone. That way, you can say you didn't want to walk home in the dark."

"Which would be absolutely true. You've clearly got this well thought out, so *ja*, I'd be happy to ride home with you, David Yoder."

His grin lost its edge of cockiness and became honestly happy. "*Gut.* I'll see you in the lane, then."

"Before the Millers leave."

Still smiling, he tipped his head toward the

house. "Sounds like they're getting ready for supper. *Kumm mit?*"

He walked her in, causing not a few speculative glances and nudges among the *Youngie* and even a few who weren't so young. And if Adam Miller was among them, well, she couldn't help that.

If she wanted to go home with someone else, that was absolutely none of his business.

———

"DAVE'S A FAST WORKER," Zach observed to Adam as they found places in the big sitting room, where chairs had been set out in a ring so that people could eat off plates in their laps. "If he was that good at cutting and roping, we'd be done in half the time."

Adam watched out of the corner of his eye as David gestured for Kate to precede him in the food line. The long kitchen table now held leftovers from lunch, with the addition of big bowls of chips and dip, plus hamburgers that the bishop had been grilling out in the backyard. Adam took a big bite of his cheeseburger to prevent himself from speaking.

"Then again, we've grown up with most of the girls around here," Zach said thoughtfully through his own massive mouthful of burger. "Can't blame him for trying, I guess."

"Seems silly," Adam said thickly.

"Why? Because she's leaving in a couple of days?"

He swallowed. "Take it from me, a long distance relationship doesn't work."

"It didn't work for *you*," his brother corrected him. "Doesn't mean it won't work for Dave. Kate's a nice girl. If she likes him, he's a lucky guy."

"Shows what you know." Adam put down his half-devoured burger. He must not be as hungry as he thought. Socializing tired him and Zach out, unlike Malena, who seemed to gather more energy the bigger the crowd was. "She lied."

"She wasn't the only one. So did her sister."

"But she *actively* lied."

"Uh-huh. And you told me last night she

apologized. Asked you to forgive her. Have you?"

A man could only take so much, even from his favorite brother. "I've already had sufficient preaching for today, *denki*."

"Not preaching," Zach said easily. "Just asking a question."

"It's none of your business."

"Ain't you fit to be tied." Zach got up. "Think I'll see what Ruby's dishing up."

Bereft, Adam knew he'd have to ask forgiveness of his brother now, too. Zach wasn't a tempery man, but he did silently expect to be treated as respectfully as he treated others. There was no excuse for snapping his head off.

Unerringly, his gaze found Kate in a chattering circle seated near the front door. Her companions included Susan Bontrager, Simeon King, and—his grouchy mood soured even further—Andrew King. Zach was talking to Ruby as she cut a piece of pie for him, so he couldn't even soothe his irritation by ambling over and saying he was sorry. In fact, there was nothing he could do but take himself off. He carried his plate out on the wraparound porch to finish his hamburger and tried to find some solace in watching the stars prick out in the velvet sky, one by one.

After the clatter of dishes died down, he heard Ruby, their hostess, choose the opening song. He slouched in and took a chair close to the back door. That way, he could be one of the first to leave. He'd be ahead of his siblings, and more important, ahead of all the departing buggies, driven by young men who had been brave enough to ask a girl if he could take her home, and lucky enough to have been accepted.

They probably wouldn't notice a single lonely figure walking in the dark, anyway.

Chapter 10

IT WAS AS THOUGH she'd developed a sixth sense where Adam was concerned. Certain animals like bats and dolphins, Kate had learned during her voracious reading of library books about animals as a child, located landmarks and food by echolocation. She wasn't emitting sounds, but even when she wasn't looking at him, she had no trouble locating him. When he slipped out on the porch for some time alone. When he came back in. And when he chose "How Great Thou Art," a fast hymn familiar to the *Youngie* in many Amish communities, her senses tingled as she sang the words, trying to divine what had spoken to him about this particular song.

She wasn't likely to learn the answer, though.

The evening ended early, around nine o'clock, with everyone fully aware of the day ahead of them tomorrow. Kate slipped out with some of the other girls. Rebecca Miller, of course, climbed into Noah King's buggy with barely a teasing remark to be heard among the other young men. Malena accepted a ride home from Cal Yoder, and in the storm of jokes and teasing and surprise, Kate was able to slip away to the bottom of the lawn to wait for his brother David. With any luck, no one would be able to make her out in the dark and they'd both be spared the good-natured teasing that the young men, at least, dreaded.

At which point the sixth sense she'd developed abruptly failed her.

She leaned on a tree and nearly jumped out of her skin when it spoke. "What brings you out in the dark?"

"Adam!" she gasped, one hand over her racing heart. "You scared me half to death."

He stepped out of the shadow behind the aspen. "You look like you're hiding," he said, apparently not aware that she could say the same about him.

"I'm not hiding. I—I'm waiting."

"For a ride?" he said in such amazed tones it was all she could do not to take offense.

"What if I am?"

It seemed she had taken him aback just a bit. Good.

"None of my business, I suppose," he said.

"Is that what you're doing out here? Minding your own business?"

"*Ja*, unlike some."

She didn't need to put up with this. "I'll leave you to it, then."

Her skirts rustled as she stepped away and he made a convulsive movement, as though he had reached for her. "Kate, wait."

She stopped, half of her thrilling at the sound of her name on his lips, the other half aware that a buggy was coming down the lane. *Don't let it be David. Not yet.*

"*Ja?*"

"I just wanted to say— I mean, I know you

think I'm mad at you. But I wanted to tell you—"

"Whoa. Kate?" The buggy came to a stop, and Kate recognized David's voice. "Is that you?"

"*Ja*, it's me." In a quieter voice, she said over her shoulder, "*Guder nacht*, Adam."

But to her surprise, as she walked away toward the glow of the buggy lamps, she heard him coming along behind her. And before she could do much more than wonder what on earth he was up to, he went around the back of David's buggy while she went around the horse's head to the passenger side.

He got there first. Bracing both hands on either side of the open door, he leaned in to talk to David, effectively blocking her from getting in.

"Looking for a ride home, Miller?" David said, his voice tinged with laughter. "I'm sure there's a girl in a buggy coming along any minute."

"Very funny," Adam said. "Look, Dave, I need to talk to Kate. All right if I walk her home?"

Well, if that didn't beat all! The nerve of him,

to ignore her for days on end, and then when someone else took notice, to wake up and decide he wanted to speak to her after all!

"Don't ask me," David said, a little blankly. "Ask Kate. She's standing right there."

Adam released the door frame and turned in her direction. She could hear another buggy coming, and if they didn't move, they'd not only block the lane, they'd be fodder for jokes for days.

"Kate?" Adam said. "I really need to talk to you."

"I'm staying at your house." She slipped past him and climbed nimbly into the buggy. "You can talk to me anytime. Just not now. All right, David."

Without another word, David clucked to the horse and the buggy jerked into motion. Adam stepped back and faded into the dark so completely it was almost as though he hadn't been there at all.

"I hope it wasn't something important," David said as they rattled down the lane. His buggy was clearly a hand-me-down, but it was well looked after. Overlaying the smell of old leather was the scent of some kind of cleanser, along with saddle soap, which told her he had taken the time to polish up his buggy and tack on the off chance she might agree to a ride home with him.

It felt nice to have a man go out of his way to try to please her. It was also a very new feeling. At home, there had been a buzzing crowd of boys around Elizabeth since the day she started school. Not too many of them ever turned to look Kate's way, and even fewer offered her a ride home after singing. She could count them on one hand.

"I don't know," she said now, in answer to his question. "Adam never got around to telling me what he wanted. But his timing could have been better."

David laughed. "I'm glad you picked me and the buggy instead of him and shank's mare. It's not often anybody gets the better of the Miller boys."

"This isn't a competition," she pointed out, trying not to sound nettled. "I'm glad you asked me. It's nice to get to know some of the *Youngie* here."

He turned the horse on to the highway for the half mile or so to the Circle M gate, with its crossbar bearing the ranch's brand.

"I hear you're leaving sometime this week," he said. "Maybe my timing could have been better, too."

"I'm not sure when," she admitted. "It turns out the King brothers are heading back to Amity this week as well. The Millers think it would be a *gut* idea if I went with them. I'd have company until Denver, at least, but we'll still have to coordinate tickets and all that."

"You'd go with them?"

Why did he sound so surprised? "Sure. They seem like *gut* company. It's a long trip to take alone. Having friends along for even a third of the way is a gift."

"But … three men and you, all by yourself? Is Rebecca going?"

"I don't think so. Why would she?"

He turned in at the Circle M lane, and a glance at him in the yellow light of the buggy lamps showed his brows drawn together.

"I don't know," he said at last. "It just don't seem proper, I guess. Becoming of a church member. That Andrew has quite the reputation."

She couldn't help a snort. "I'm pretty sure I'm safe from him and his reputation. He hasn't said more than hello to me in all the time I've been here."

"But if Noah is dating Rebecca and Simeon is interested in Susan Bontrager, that leaves Andrew at loose ends. And there's a lot of hours between here and Denver."

This was *not* the conversation she had expected to have with David Yoder tonight. "Trust me—even if he wanted to take me to dinner in the fanciest restaurant in Denver, I would find a way to be unavailable." She laughed at the thought. "You don't have to worry, David. Honest."

He drew up in the yard, at the bottom of the steps to the house. A hurricane lamp glowed in the living room window, and another had been left burning at the top of the stairs. The bedroom windows were all dark.

She was barely twenty-three years old, and she had never been this alone with a man before. Or maybe it was the vast crags of the mountains stretching up behind the house, blotting out the glow of stars in the singing silence, that made her feel that way.

"*Denki* for the ride," she said, reaching for the sliding door.

"Don't go yet," he begged. "I was just thinking it's a nice night. We might take a walk by the river or something."

You've probably found your way home from here a hundred times in the dark, she heard herself saying to Adam in her memory. No way did she want to overlay that memory with one of David, nice as he was, tripping over rocks and frightening nocturnal animals as they made their way down to that gravel bar. Besides, if he was so concerned about her reputation, he ought to have suggested that they sit together on the porch, or even in the living room.

"We have to be up early," she said. She jumped down and looked across at him. "I'll see you tomorrow, okay?"

"*Ja.* I'll look forward to that. *Guder nacht,* Kate."

"*Guder nacht.*"

He waited politely until she reached the

door and turned to wave. Then he guided the horse around and jogged off down the lane, his harness jingling until he rounded the curve and she couldn't hear it anymore over the sound of the river below.

"You should have gone for that walk."

For the second time tonight, she gasped and whirled. And there he was again, leaning on the deck rail, hands clasped. He might have been carved out of wood, for all the sound he'd made.

"How did you get here so fast?"

"Shortcut. Came in the back way."

"What on earth—were you spying on us?"

"I do live here," Adam pointed out.

"But—but—" A thousand words crowded her tongue, and not a single sensible syllable came out. She controlled herself with an effort.

"Don't worry, I didn't see anything I shouldn't have."

"There wasn't anything to see!" Honestly, the nerve of him. "How fast do you think I am, Adam Miller? I'm not about to kiss a man I hardly know the first time he takes me home."

"I guess I don't know that for sure." Was that laughter lurking at the back of his voice? "The girl who's been writing to me all this time never said a word about dating other guys."

"I didn't. Haven't been, I mean."

"But Elizabeth has."

And there she was again, stepping between them as neatly as if she was real.

"*Ja*, she has. But I couldn't very well put that in the letters, could I?"

"No, I suppose not. Not until this last one." A pause. "So, no kiss good night, huh? Not even a tiny peck on the cheek?"

"*Neh*," she told him firmly. "Not that it's any of your business."

He cantered past that without even noticing. "What did you talk about?"

"As I just said, it's none of your business."

"Come on. It couldn't have been *that* personal. Not in ten minutes."

Drat him for being right. "I told him I might be leaving with the King brothers later in the week. After turnout." She frowned.

"And?"

"Adam, do you think it's unbecoming for a woman to travel alone with them? The Kings?"

He straightened at the rail. The faint glow of

the lamp behind the window lit one side of his face just enough for her to see him, like an outline in the dark. "I don't think so. *Neh*. They're *gut* men. One of them is probably going to be my brother-in-law, if this keeps up. Why would you ask that?"

"David seemed to think I was in some kind of danger from the middle one. Andrew."

One broad shoulder lifted in a shrug. "He'll flirt if you give him the chance, but I don't think any girl is in danger from more than getting her heart broke. His brothers would set him straight if he put a toe over the line with you. Sim has pretty strict views about what's becoming and what's not, if what Noah tells me is true."

She took a deep breath of cool night air, as though David's strange take on the situation had constricted her lungs in some way.

"*Gut. Denki* for telling me that."

"Would it have stopped you from going?"

"I don't think so. They're my brothers in Christ."

"Not the Kings. I meant David's opinion of your going with them."

"Oh." She thought about it for a moment. "*Neh*, it wouldn't. I hardly know him. He doesn't know me. It was just an odd thing to say … in the ten minutes we had to talk to each other." She tilted her head to look at him. "Speaking of, what was it you wanted to talk to me about before?"

In the silence she could hear the whisper of the river down in the water meadows, and a creak that must be two pines rubbing together. She was tempted to ask again, then changed her mind. Instead, she waited.

At length he removed his hat and ruffled up his hair, as though it would help him say what he wanted to say. When he put it back on, he said, "I'm not angry with you. Not anymore."

"But you were."

"*Ja*. Can you blame me?"

She shook her head. "I would have been angry with me, too. So … does this mean you've forgiven me?"

"I have," he said slowly, as though he wasn't quite sure yet. "Staying angry and resentful isn't going to harm anyone but me. Elizabeth is—was—a dream I didn't want to wake up from.

And she's not here to say whether she's sorry or not."

"She had the chance," Kate said. "But she decided not to use that train ticket. I think she was afraid of what Mark would think if she did. I can hardly blame her. He's crazy about her, but still. He wouldn't have liked it."

"And she didn't think a phone call or a letter would have done?"

"We wrote a letter," she said in a small voice. "That's the one you got the other day. I was going to write again with the news of her getting engaged to Mark. And that would have been the end of it. Except—"

"I sent the ticket." He nodded, as though the pieces had finally fallen into place.

"More than that. Your mother wrote to Carrie Miller, and she stopped Elizabeth in town because she thought the two of you were special friends, and Elizabeth wanted to order a white groom's cake ... and Carrie thought she meant you. Oh my, it was a mess. Lizzie was so angry with me."

"Why?" He sounded honestly curious. "None of that had anything to do with you."

"It was still my fault. For what was in the letters. She told me I had to do something, and fast."

"So that's why you came in person."

"Not because of her. But because I felt responsible. I kept up the correspondence for a year and a half when she might have just let it go. But I—"

This time it was he who waited in the blowing silence of the night. For her to find the words.

"I enjoyed your letters so much," she finally concluded. "It was wicked. I know that now. But I couldn't wait to read them. You have a gift, Adam. For making life just walk off the page."

He made a sound that could have been a chuckle. "My Daadi Glick used to say that. Mamm's father. They moved away from the valley before I was born. But after they came to visit every year, I'd write and tell him all about what the horses and cattle were doing and what flowers were up. Daadi was interested in that kind of thing, too. He wasn't much of a rancher, but he liked nature, and birds. Stuff like that."

"Have you ever thought of writing for *The Budget*? Or *Family Life*?"

This time he did chuckle. "Not even once."

"Maybe you should. I think people would like your views on ranch life. It's not the same as farming, is it?"

"Not by a long shot. But why would anyone care what I think?" He sounded as though he really wanted to know.

"Because there aren't so many scribes out there who live on a working ranch. Even a description of a single day is not exactly like putting up pickle relish, is it?"

"I've never tried to put up pickle relish."

She poked him in the ribs for being smart with her, and he laughed.

"And the way you fold in your thoughts about *Gott*'s creation, and the way people are with one another, your humor ... well, I think they'd accept letters from you. My cousin's wife Emma writes for both. And she has a novel out, too—*The Friendship Quilt*."

"That's your cousin's wife?" He sounded as amazed as if he'd never considered before that real people held the pens that created letters and manuscripts to be published. "They have that book in Yoder's Variety Store."

"The bishop gave her permission to publish it because her husband was in a terrible accident and couldn't work. He's mending now, and she's got a contract to write another one."

"Huh."

He sounded as if he might actually think about it. Well, she knew when to sow a seed and when to water it. And when to walk away and leave it to grow by itself.

"I'm going in," she said. "I think I hear a buggy in the lane. Whoever it is, I don't want them to think I'm watching for them."

"Me either. I'm going to check the cows. *Guder nacht.*"

"*Guder nacht*, Adam."

And when she snuggled down under the quilt his sister had made, for the first time since she'd arrived on the Circle M, she fell at once into a deep and untroubled sleep.

Chapter 11

FOUR O'CLOCK CAME EARLY with a knock on Kate's door and a cheery "Time to get up!" from Naomi Miller. Kate dressed quickly in her taupe dress and no apron, in case, as Rebecca had explained in the corral, "the wind catches it and it spooks the cattle." Under it would go the same pair of borrowed blue jeans, and over it a camp jacket until the day warmed up. She coiled her hair tightly and tied a *Duchly* over it. A starched white *Kapp* would never survive the day even if it managed to stay on.

She and the twins helped Naomi make and serve the food—platters of scrambled eggs, bacon, thick slices of ham, roasted potatoes with onions and chiles, and coffee by the gallon. They had a crowd for breakfast—the Miller family and their hired hands, the King brothers, the bishop's family, and one or two of their *Englisch* neighbors who were pitching in as thanks for the Millers having done the same for them a week or two before.

The sun was peeping over the serrated peaks of the mountains when Reuben gathered them all in the yard to assign jobs. The most experienced were to ride alongside the river of cattle, including Adam and his brothers. "We'll need to be careful on the highway," Reuben reminded them. "We've got seven miles of flat pavement and two hundred unpredictable animals. Rebecca, Joel, and Kate, I want you on the highway directing traffic at our gate."

The almost nine-year-old whooped at being given a job and made his adoptive grandfather smile.

"We'll try to keep the cattle to the right lane so trucks and vehicles can get through on the other side. Malena and Ruby, you'll go on ahead to the turnoff at the allotments and do the same.

Close up behind them and once the cattle are through the first gate, close it behind you and watch for runaways."

"It's all right," Rebecca assured her as she helped Kate saddle Marigold while Daniel and Joel saddled their horses. "You may be a new rider, but you're with experienced people. Joel may be young, but he did well at roundup last fall, so that's why Dat is giving him responsibility now." She scooped up a man's straw hat from a peg as they led the horses out. "You'll need this again, once the sun comes up."

Adam's letter describing turnout had been wonderful, but it didn't come close to the reality of it. The herd of cattle, brown and white, mothers and calves, bawling and lowing, lumbered toward the gate across the acres of the field in a flowing river of movement and noise. Kate lost her courage for a second and nearly turned her horse's head to gallop back up the lane to the barn. The only thing holding her there was that she had no practice in galloping and would fall off for sure and certain.

She, Joel, and Rebecca took up positions on the county highway while Zach opened the big gate that closed off the home fields a mile from the house. The cattle flowed out of it, Amish cowboys on their horses flanking and trailing the herd, yipping and whistling to keep the animals going in the same direction.

"What's going on here?" hollered a man in a small truck pulling a travel trailer, slowing to an unwilling stop.

"Dad, it's cowboys!" His son hung out the window, eyes alight with joy. "Real cowboys on a cattle drive—and there's a kid like me!"

"Yeah, well, they're really in the way," his father retorted.

Joel nudged his horse closer. "You can get through," he called. "Use the other lane and go slow."

"What if an eighteen-wheeler is in that lane, sonny?" the man demanded.

"Then you yield and wait," Rebecca informed him with a big smile. "We'll be out of your way soon."

The *Englisch* driver waited not very patiently as the cattle poured out on the highway like milk out of a pail. And then the cowboys went to work, narrowing the stream and getting it flowing along in the right-hand lane, their horses acting as both squeeze and dam. By this time three more cars were waiting behind the *Englisch* man, including a big red truck with a row of lights on a bar atop the cab.

"Rebecca!" hollered the driver. "Guess I picked the wrong day to go to town."

"Hi, Chance. Hey, Clint. Nothing is open in town. It's only six o'clock."

"Need some help? We can break out the four-wheelers in ten minutes."

"We're good, thanks," she called back. "But you might ride point for this travel trailer. He's worried about all the diesel rigs running up and down this highway."

"Yep, I heard those varmints were a problem. Broke into someone's henhouse just last week."

Joel cackled like a startled hen, and Kate gathered that eighteen-wheelers didn't happen along very often on this particular road. The red truck pulled out and waved the travel trailer in behind, and off the caravan of vehicles went at roughly the same speed as the cattle.

"You know those folks, I assume?" she asked.

"They own the Rocking Diamond next

door." Rebecca reined Juniper into her original position in the middle of the lane. "Dude ranch. Tons of money. They wanted to buy Sara's farm at Christmas and she said no. I don't think Taylor Madison—those boys' mother—has gotten over it yet."

"Why did she want Sara's farm?"

"We thought it was for the hay. Turns out the farm backs on to BLM land and they wanted to turn it into a trail ride business for tourists. People don't say no to Taylor Madison very often."

Joel turned in his saddle. "Mamm says being told no is like cod liver oil. It's not much fun, but it's good for you."

Kate had to laugh, and then a calf juked across the road and headed for the trees on the other side.

"Oh no, you don't." Rebecca and Juniper raced after it and got it turned around before a car came along and didn't see it in time. It rejoined the herd, bawling for its mother.

They had two more calves to chase—well, Rebecca and Joel did—Kate had all she could do to stay in the saddle and be a roadblock. David

Yoder followed the last of the cattle out of the gate and closed it with a clang. He was already covered in mud, but he grinned at Kate.

"That does it for the easy part," he said. "I'll give you a hand back here. We don't want them bunching up and spilling into the other lane."

She wouldn't have believed this congenial young man was the same one who just yesterday disapproved of her traveling with his spiritual brothers in the church. But there was no time to think about any of that. She had too much to do keeping the cows and calves moving at just the right speed, she and Joel falling back to keep them from running home while David and Rebecca kept them in the lane as well as they could. Sometimes traffic just came to a halt while cows walked between cars to eat some attractive grass. Sometimes a stranger was rude and honked the horn, scaring a calf into a run that one of the cowboys had to head off. But for the most part, any traffic they encountered was made up of neighbors and longtime residents of the valley.

"They've been living alongside spring turnout for fifty years," Rebecca said cheerfully, waving someone on. "But they know money comes into the valley when beef goes out to people's tables. Everyone understands."

As the four of them approached the turnoff to the allotment, still bringing up the rear, Kate looked up past the big open gate to a meadow on the rising slope to the west. Cattle were streaming up a dirt track, and overflowing it into the grass. And there was Adam, waving his straw hat as he caught sight of them. She waved back, but he was too busy keeping the cattle moving to wait for them.

"I've got the gate," Malena called, as she and Ruby moved in from their posts on the highway and the cars and pickups that had been waiting and watching the spectacle got rolling once again.

The heavy rail gate clanged shut behind them, and Marigold moved under Kate as though this were the most familiar ride in the world. While the twins and David and Ruby dashed after the occasional runaway confused about where its mother was in the melee, Kate and Joel rode along behind the herd, watchful for the signs of a calf about to make a break for it.

Six more gates had to be opened and closed, so as the newest member of the crew, that became her job. And as the last one clanged shut behind the herd, she realized they were out in open country now, on what Reuben Miller had called his allotment. These must be the foothills, the grassy, pine-forested shoulders of land that preceded the craggy rise in altitude toward the mountains.

"Beautiful, ain't so?" Adam's voice made her turn in her saddle, and Marigold shifted in case that meant she wanted to work.

Kate patted the horse's neck to reassure her that she was just an observer, mostly. "It is, for sure and certain," she said. "What happens now?"

"Now they're free." He rested both gloved hands on the saddle horn, reins secure in his grip. "We did our best to make sure they mothered up as we came through the collection pens."

"Mothered up?"

"That's when the calves find their mothers," Joel piped in.

Adam nodded. "The pairs will stay together all summer, until we bring them down at roundup, around Labor Day."

"And then?"

"Then we separate out the ones going to market. They have to be weaned, but at the same time we want them weighing what they should to fetch the best price."

"But up here, don't they get lost?"

"There are experienced cows in the mix. The newer mothers tend to follow them. And if they don't, we know all their hiding places in gulleys and coulees, don't we, Joel?"

The boy nodded solemnly.

"Cows don't stick to their own allotments, that's for sure. That's why in the fall they get sorted down there in the collection meadows."

"By brand?"

"*Ja.* You learn quick."

"I heard the men talking on branding day. I didn't want to watch that part, though."

"Can't blame you. But it's the easiest way to identify an animal. We don't have a problem with cattle rustling here, but in other places I've heard they do. Brands help with the sorting."

"I thought rustling was just in books."

Adam shook his head, eyes always on the cattle, always alert. "I suppose it's human nature to want to get something the easy way." He grinned. "But the Siksika Valley outfits all know one another. It's pretty hard to get away with anything, never mind riding off with another outfit's animals." His gaze swung back to her. "And here you are, riding off with my hat. Where'd you get that?"

She had reached up with a gloved hand to take it off before she realized he was teasing. "Rebecca plunked it on my head when we left the barn. She was right. It's bright up here."

"Altitude," he said. "The air is thinner, so your skin will burn faster. Keep it on. It suits you."

He wheeled Delphinium around after a calf dodging for the pines. Joel leaned forward and his horse responded to cut off the calf's escape. She watched the two of them go back to work.

His hat suited her?

"Glory be," she murmured to Marigold,

whose ears swiveled toward her. "I think he really has forgiven me."

———

WHILE IT WAS tradition during roundup to be prepared with supply packs in case the weather turned and they had to spend the night on the mountain, during spring turnout it was different. Today, Adam had in his pack a Thermos flask and his share of the large midmorning snack that his mother had sent along with all her offspring.

While they relaxed and enjoyed the sight of the mother cows and their calves getting used to their newfound freedom, he and his siblings handed around homemade doughnuts, coffee cake, and elk sausage rolls, along with slightly squashed paper cups of coffee. After the size of the breakfast he'd enjoyed this morning, Adam wouldn't have believed that he would be ready for a snack. But there was something about mountain air and hard work that made a man ready for a doughnut no matter what the time of day.

Kate was wandering along the bank of a tiny creek no more than a foot across, bending to peer into the water as though she thought trout might be hiding there. He fetched a second cup of coffee and a doughnut, and ambled over to join her.

"Looking for a place to cast a line?"

She looked up in surprise. "Are there trout at this altitude?"

"Not here. But in other places, *ja*, especially in the alpine meadows. You can find browns up there."

"It's hard to believe. *Denki*." She took the doughnut and bit into it with a sigh of pleasure. "I suppose they don't have to come from the ocean to spawn, do they?"

"They're like us. Spending their lives in the high country."

She sipped the coffee while the spring wind made her skirts flap around the tops of her borrowed boots. Flakes of drying mud sifted to the grass. "So now what happens?"

He straightened from his contemplation of the creek. Did she mean ... now that the howling loss inside him had reduced itself to a muttering growl? Or that sometimes he forgot altogether that he was supposed to be angry with her?

"Do we follow the cows up higher to make sure they don't hurt themselves?"

Oh.

"They're on their own now." His cheeks burned, and not from the intense sun, either. "We'll let the horses rest and graze a little longer. Then we'll head back. Mamm is expecting us all for dinner."

"Then I suppose it would be a *gut* opportunity for me to stop ogling the creek and make some arrangements with the King brothers. We should settle on a day and buy train tickets."

"Or you could just leave it up to them. They'll buy your ticket at the same time, and tell you when you're leaving."

She smiled, a little self-consciously. "Are you telling me I'm bossy? Trying to direct the men when it's not my place?"

The thought hadn't crossed his mind. "It takes longer for three men to make a decision than one woman. Best stay out of the process.

Besides, you're not in such a hurry to leave, are you?"

As she bent to examine a small cluster of purple lupine no bigger than Adam's hand, her face was hidden by his hat. "I'm not in a hurry, but I don't want to outstay my *wilkumm*, either. Are these lupine?"

"*Ja*. They never get very big up here, unlike at home. Weather's hard on them up here in the open. But small as they are, they bloom with all their might once they get some sun."

When she straightened, she was smiling. "Like me."

The sun had brought out the freckles across her nose. How had he never noticed the way a smile changed her whole face? Had she not smiled since she'd been here, or had he simply refused to look at her because she wasn't Elizabeth?

"How do you mean?" he asked.

"I feel like I'm in the sun." She lifted her hands just a little, as if to hold the mountain sunshine in her palms.

"You don't have sun in Pennsylvania?"

"Well, let's put it this way—if my sister were

here, right now, nobody would be thinking about the sun. Or rather, it would be like she *was* the sun, and everyone would revolve around her. Like the planets do."

Adam blinked, a little taken aback. But now that he thought about it, he had to agree. "I remember many a singing and baseball game," he said on a note of discovery, "that were like that." He hadn't noticed because he'd been at her side.

"Not that I blame her," she said quickly, as though he might have got the wrong impression. "It's just the way she is. And I'm not jealous."

"I never thought you were. It's just … the truth."

Because he'd been one of those planets, revolving around her, doing little things for her, bringing her gifts, all in the hopes that doing so would keep her attention on him. "But the truth is," he mused, half to himself, "that the sun doesn't need the planets. It does what it does, with or without them."

After a moment, she said, "Everyone needs

someone. A parent, a sibling, a partner. No one wants to be alone in the world."

"My brother Joshua discovered that the hard way." Adam found him in the crowd, one arm slung over his grazing horse's neck while he talked with the bishop. "He was bound and determined to jump the fence. But once he met Sara, he couldn't do it without her and Nathan. And she wouldn't go. One fence jumper saved the other, and now they've both joined church."

"They seem happy," she offered, following his gaze.

"It's been a long time since I saw Josh honestly happy. He's like a different man. Settled in his heart. No more revolving around suns that don't care about him." He smiled at his awful metaphor for Seattle, the big city that had been Joshua's goal for so long. "I should do the same."

When he glanced at Kate to see why she hadn't replied, he found her gazing at him, a tiny pleat between her brows. Something like a thrill, or a shiver, arrowed through him. When was the last time anyone had studied him this intently? Had anyone, ever?

For the first time, he saw how deep and striking the blue of her eyes was, starred with long lashes.

"Kate!" someone shouted.

The moment broke as she whirled to meet the approaching Malena. "Come on, we're going to walk up to the spring. Adam, you too. Stretch those legs before we have to get back in the saddle."

"I'm always in the saddle," Adam protested mildly, but he followed them anyway.

He'd seen the spring—the genesis of this little creek—bubbling out of its hiding place in the rocks a hundred times. But Kate hadn't. Someone who had a knack for studying the little bits of beauty in the high country would probably find it as pretty and refreshing as he did.

Would Elizabeth have walked up to the granite outcrops to do the same?

Because if, as Kate had said, Elizabeth didn't like getting messy, he very much doubted she would even have come along today. He just couldn't picture her learning to ride a horse. Or putting on jeans under her dress, getting splashed to the knees in drying mud and manure from the ride.

No, Elizabeth would have stayed at the house and offered to help Mamm and the other neighbor women. When he arrived at the end of the day, there she would be, looking breathtakingly beautiful in her pristine white *Kapp*, with not a red-gold hair out of place. Smelling of something good, like cake frosting. Not horse sweat.

Up ahead, Kate threw back her head and laughed at something Malena said. Adam picked up his pace. He didn't want to be left behind—or to miss the moment when she got her first glimpse of the spring.

WITH THE WINDOWS open to catch the last of the day's warmth before the sun dropped behind the pines, Naomi and Sadie Wengerd heard the approaching cavalcade long before they saw them.

"Here they come," she said to her friend. "Dinner in an hour?"

"I think so." Sadie opened the door of the propane oven to check the ranks of baked potatoes, oiled and salted and wrapped in foil. "These need another fifteen minutes, and they'll stay warm a long time."

In keeping with tradition, Naomi's trademark elk stew once again bubbled outside on the deck on a big, one-burner propane cooker. With the potatoes baked and "smashed," as Joshua put it, her hungry guests could ladle stew over them and fill their plates with creamed corn and green bean casserole with bacon and onions, plus all the pickles and jellied salads their stomachs could hold.

No one ever went hungry at the big dinner after turnout. The *gut Gott* provided with a generous hand, and every family brought something to contribute along with their labor.

And here they came, riding across the big home field and into the barn through the back gate. The guest horses were turned out into the paddock, still tacked up but free to graze and rest after their exertions. She could picture her family, weary and covered in mud, but still taking the time to remove saddle and tack, and brush their horses down before turning them out to graze on the sweet grass of the meadows.

Denkes, mei Vater, for bringing them safe home again.

Kate Weaver climbed the stairs up to the deck, already part of the crowd even though she hadn't yet been here a week. Naomi took in her stiff gait, the taupe dress nearly unrecognizable with mud and sweat, the hair escaping from under her *Duchly*. But before she could cross the wide deck and suggest a change of clothes, Malena and Rebecca, both in the same disarray, hustled her inside.

Her *gut Dochsdere*. They would look after the greenhorn.

And here was her husband, looking tired but still with the spark of pleasure in his eyes as he caught sight of her. He made his way over to her through the crowd dispersing itself on the picnic benches and along the railings. He didn't kiss her, but she could see perfectly well he wanted to.

She brushed dried mud off the shoulders of his shirt like a caress. She never permitted herself to think of everything that could go wrong in the high country during turnout. Calves stuck in barbed-wire fences. Horses losing their footing on crumbly scree and tossing a rider. Inexperienced help not latching a gate securely and cattle streaming onto someone else's land. Calves and horses darting out into traffic on the highway.

Since she could do not one thing to prevent any of that, she left it all in *Gott*'s capable hands, and gave thanks to Him when Reuben and her children returned to her, muddy but unscathed.

"How did it go?"

Reuben's cheeks creased in a smile. "Our greenhorns did well. I've said before that Joel has a knack for ranch work. Under Rebecca's *gut* management, he and Kate Weaver did traffic duty without a single mishap."

She raised her eyebrows.

"Other than the usual," he amended.

Joel flew into his mother's arms, talking a mile a minute about his adventures with the cattle while Daniel, smiling at his bride and adopted son, joined in to fill in the details.

"And on the allotment?" Naomi asked. "How did Kate manage her first ride?"

"She's going to be sore tomorrow," he predicted. "Some liniment tonight wouldn't go amiss."

"I'll make sure she gets some. And … our Adam?"

Reuben knew better than to test her patience by pretending not to know what she meant. "Something has happened there."

"Has it, now?" Naomi tilted her head so she wouldn't miss a thing, from a note in his voice to a twitch of an eyebrow.

"Don't get your hopes up, but … there is a change in our boy. I believe he has forgiven her for not being her sister."

"Or for writing her sister's letters?"

"I think it's bigger than the letters." Reuben leaned closer. "He actually brought her coffee and a doughnut up in the meadow."

That was news. It had to mean something.

"Naomi Miller, you've got that look in your eye."

"I think the *gut Gott* has something in mind for our son," she said.

"Then you should leave it up to Him."

"Every child of His has a pair of hands for

His work," she told him blithely. "I can only obey where I'm led. And right now I must give that stew a stir. The potatoes will come out of the oven any minute."

"Don't change the subject," he warned her, trying not to laugh.

She could never put anything past him. Instead, she stole a kiss. "It's all one subject," she told him, and went to rescue her good spatula before one of the *Kinner* decided they needed to contribute a mud pie to dinner.

Chapter 12

KATE HAD BEEN dirty plenty of times—putting in the garden, mucking out horse stalls, cleaning the chicken coop—but she had not fully realized the blessing of hot water before this. There was no time for baths or showers. Instead, she and the Miller twins filled big enamel bowls with steaming water and got busy with soap and facecloth. She changed into a clean green dress and black kitchen apron, then re-coiled her hair, smoothing it under her heart-shaped *Kapp* and pinning it with three straight pins—one on top, one each on the sides. Cleanliness was next to godliness for a *gut* reason. It went a long way toward making her feel fit for the company of God's people again.

And she had her reward. Out on the deck, when she caught Adam's eye quite by accident, his up-and-down look of surprise made a blush burn into her face. Oh, but she couldn't think that way. Just because he'd brought her coffee and a doughnut this morning didn't mean anything but that he'd forgiven her. That was all.

All right, that was everything.

Her heart was as guilty of running away with her as any horse could be, the way it kicked into a gallop at the sight of him.

Shaking her head at herself, she smiled at Ruby Wengerd and joined the line with her, picking up a plate and cutlery and then trying not to overload it with all the wonderful food laid out on the long table. They sure knew how to eat, these ranch folks. Then again, most Amish did. Hard work and long days required sustenance. Throw in rugged country and runaway calves, and there was every reason to ladle a big helping of stew on a smashed potato and not feel one bit guilty about it.

She and Ruby found seats on either side of Rebecca Miller and Noah King, and in a moment they were joined by Simeon and a girl a year or two older than Kate. She wore a burgundy dress with a cape and apron of the same color, the way the *Maedeln* did here in Montana, instead of the contrasting black worn back east.

"I'm Susan Bontrager," the girl said, handing Simeon the salt and pepper shakers without being asked. "We met on Sunday."

"I remember," Kate said. But before she could say more, Andrew King slid in on her other side.

"Is this seat taken?"

"It is now," she said dryly. "What would you have done if I'd said yes?"

"Finders keepers," he said, and shoveled in a mouthful of elk stew. "How was the ride?"

She and Noah told their companions all about the experience of being a greenhorn, since like her, the King family didn't have a ranch background. Everything was new to both of them. New, and exciting, and a little bit scary.

"You both did really well," Rebecca assured

them. "And Kate, I was proud of you. For a person who had never been on a horse before Saturday, you remembered most of what Malena and I taught you."

"You mean Marigold did," Kate said ruefully. "She did all the work. The only thing I managed was to stick in the saddle and hang on for dear life."

Andrew laughed. "I'd have liked to see that. Maybe next year, when my leg is healed up, I can help out."

"You'll get plenty of opportunity to help on Aendi Annie's place," Simeon reminded him. "If you're not coming to Colorado, then you'll have to do the finish work on Mamm and Dat's house. That'll save Noah and me a lot of time in August. Dat thinks we'll be able to take off the hay early."

Kate put down her fork. "You're not going to Colorado?" she asked Andrew. "Yesterday after church, I thought that was the plan."

He shook his head and indicated his leg, stuck out straight where he sat on the end of the bench. "I won't be much use to King Carpentry like this. We decided last night that I should stay behind and work on the house."

"Like you were supposed to do in April," Noah said.

"Right," his brother admitted.

What was the story there that they all seemed to know and weren't telling? She'd probably never find out.

"But on the good side," Andrew resumed, "Kate can have my ticket. It means you only have to buy one from Denver to Lancaster. It'll be cheaper."

"*Neh*, certainly not," Kate protested in surprise. "I can buy my own ticket."

"Already done," Simeon said, his deep voice cutting through her consternation. "We called and reserved seats for a Thursday noon departure. If you can get over to Aendi Annie's place by eight, the *Englisch* taxi is coming at eight thirty. We have to be there at least an hour in advance."

"Thursday?" Carrying a loaded plate, Adam hooked a folding chair with one booted foot and dragged it over to sit at the end of the table,

Andrew on his left and Susan on his right. "You're leaving that soon?"

Kate's feelings exactly. She'd known she was leaving this week. She'd even toyed with which day. But to have it nailed down so firmly—good grief, Thursday was only three days off! Three days left on the Circle M. Three days left to talk with Adam, to sit at a table with him, to watch him ride across the fields with the easy sway of the lifelong horseman.

Only three days!

"You don't have to go if you don't want to," Adam said, his gaze flicking up to her and back to his plate. "Train goes a couple of times a week."

"Oh, but—but—" She stopped herself with an effort. "I couldn't impose."

He shook his head. "No imposition. It's not like you're Andrew here, eating people out of house and home."

He tilted his head at Andrew's empty plate, and the latter laughed. "You've got a point there, Miller."

Kate played along. "Maybe you're right.

After all, I've been told that traveling with you boys alone isn't becoming to an Amish woman."

Three sets of cutlery were abruptly laid down. Four, if she counted Rebecca's.

"What's this, now?" Noah said, half laughing. "That's ridiculous."

"It's a fact," Adam said. "Apparently there are those in the *Gmay* who believe it."

"Nonsense," Simeon said, picking up his fork and resuming his meal. "Who said that?"

"Best not to gossip," Adam said. "But I believe the incident occurred last night."

"Incident," Susan sniffed. "Only someone who was jealous would say such a thing. There's nothing forward about an Amish woman traveling with male church members. You're a lot less likely to be bothered by *Englisch* men, for sure and certain."

"Did you have trouble along that line on the way out?" Adam asked Kate, his brows pulling together in a frown.

"Not really. I made sure I sat near *Englisch* couples who had babies, if I could, and helped the mothers if they needed it. Goodness knows

I've had lots of practice. And then, of course, between Lancaster and Pittsburgh there were several Amish families traveling, so they invited me to join them."

"Smart," Susan said. "*Gott* was looking out for you. But goodness me, don't let someone's silly opinion prevent you from traveling Thursday. Or from using Andrew's ticket. You can change the reservation name on it at the station."

There was that. It was a generous gift from the King brothers, and if she turned it down just because she didn't want to leave yet—because her heart didn't want to leave—then she would appear ungrateful.

"I'll do that," she assured Susan. It felt as though she were taking a leap from a high cliff. Once she stepped off, there was no going back. No staying. "I'm very grateful to you both for asking me along. If someone from here can give me a lift to Annie's place, I'll be there by eight."

"That's settled, then," Simeon said.

Kate willed herself not to look at Adam. Instead, she caught Rebecca gazing at her.

Puzzled. Wistful. As though she had been thinking Kate ought to stay a little longer, too. But the decision was made, and she couldn't go back on it.

So then, why did it feel as if doing the right thing had been a mistake?

After supper, the single young women wasted no time in washing the dishes so that visitors could take home clean bowls and serving spoons. "We're going to have a bonfire," Malena said, rinsing dishes as fast as Ruby could wash them. "The boys are building it down at the river."

"We might even have some singing," Rebecca said, efficiently putting away the clean dishes Kate had dried. "From memory, of course. Can't read songbooks in the dark."

"We took the songbooks down there one year," Malena explained to Kate. "What a mistake! Some of them wound up in the river, after the fire burned down and people were walking around. And people used them for seat cushions and bent them. After that Mamm said we should know them all by heart."

"Which we do, mostly," Ruby said. "And if the *Vorsinger* forgets, he makes something up."

"It sounds *wunderbaar*," Kate said. "We have bonfires at home, too, but there's no river. And certainly no stars like there are here. I've never seen anything like the night sky in Montana."

"I really don't want you to go," Rebecca said. "Are you sure you can't stay a little while longer?"

How sweet she was! "I don't think so. Like Susan said, they've already paid for part of my ticket."

"They can get a refund," Malena told her. "If you don't want to go, then don't."

She made it sound so easy. "Mamm needs me at home. We only just got the garden in before I left, but there will be weeding, and the chickens, and laundry, and—well, you know."

"But you have, what, three other sisters?" Malena said. "They can manage for a few more days, can't they?"

"Two of them are still scholars, and Elizabeth has—" She stopped, shocked at what she'd almost said. Elizabeth had often been happy to let Kate do her share because she'd had a date with a young man and had run out of time to finish. "Well, she's got wedding plans to make. It would be hard on her to do her own work, my work, plus plan a wedding on top of it."

"I suppose." Rebecca wasn't quite ready to give up, Kate could see, but neither was it her decision.

"Believe me, if I could stay, I would," she assured them. "But since I only have three days, I want to experience everything I can. Starting with our bonfire by the river."

As the ranch's neighbors trickled away after dinner, or sat in the living room visiting with Naomi and Reuben, passing Deborah around for cuddles or enjoying a second helping of coconut cream pie, the *Youngie* made their way down the path to the river in the gloaming—what Kate's mother called the golden hour, when the sun was down but the light still shone in the sky. The bonfire was already going, keeping the mosquitoes away, thank goodness. Kate hadn't noticed when she and Adam had been here the other night that there was a fire ring made of big river stones. Logs formed benches on either side of it, looking as though they'd been cast up by floodwaters and put to use.

"Does your family come down here a lot?" she asked Malena, watching Noah and Rebecca pair off, then Susan take a seat next to Simeon. Joshua and Sara sat together, little Nathan in Sara's lap. He had one fist in his mouth, his eyes big as saucers as he watched the fire.

"Every couple of weeks or so," Malena replied, stretching her sneakers out to the flames. "Dat says it's a *gut* way to remember how small we are and how big *Gott*'s creation is."

"He's right," Kate said fervently. "Who is that young man in the dark blue shirt?"

"Alden Stolzfus. He's our blacksmith. He's not able to ride with us because he's busy with his shop in town, but he's always welcome to supper and any doings afterward. After all, if it weren't for him, none of us would be riding anywhere, would we?"

Kate laughed. "I suppose not."

"I like the sound of your laugh." And here was Andrew King, plunking himself down on her left and propping his crutches against the log. "I hope it wasn't at me, trying to get down that path."

"I didn't even see you," Kate said. His face fell, as though she'd disappointed him. To make up for it, she asked, "Was it difficult?"

"Everything is difficult with a busted leg," he said. "It takes three times as long to do even the simplest thing, like get up for seconds at dinner."

"How did you break it?"

"Long story."

"The short version, then."

"I fell out of a car."

"An *Englisch* car?" she asked in surprise.

"Is there any other kind?"

He could have simply said yes. He didn't have to make her feel stupid for blurting that out.

"I suppose not." The next natural question would have been, "What made you fall out?" but at that moment Adam ambled into the firelight out of the dark and Kate forgot all about Andrew. Adam looked around for a place to sit and finally settled next to Ruby and his brother Zach on the far side of the fire.

Bother Andrew anyhow! If he hadn't parked himself and his crutches right next to her, then maybe Adam might have chosen to sit there. That made how many times today that Andrew had gotten in the way? Maybe she'd better stop being so nice to him. He could be getting ideas and that would *not* do, especially since here was David Yoder, looking at them both from the other side of the fire as if she'd just confirmed his worst predictions. The thought occurred to her that, in causing Andrew to change his mind and stay home, *Gott* might have saved her from a very aggravating trip from Libby to Denver on Thursday.

But she couldn't very well get up and sit next to Adam, now that Andrew was settled. That would be so blatantly forward that she'd be branded *fast* just as surely as any calf had been branded this week. Then again, Andrew's persistence might do just that anyway.

Well? Was she going to do what she wanted and move, if she'd be considered fast either way?

Augghhh. No, she couldn't. Slumping, a hand on the weathered wood on either side of her, she simply wasn't brave enough.

"Shall we try a song?" Malena said, and Kate could have hugged her. "How about 'Country Roads'?"

By the second verse of the familiar tune, Kate had relaxed enough to remember that it wasn't all about her. Maybe no one cared whom she sat next to. Why should they? She was a stranger who would be gone on Thursday, and the river of their lives here would close over the space she'd left as though it had never been. Which was a sad thought, even a little *hochmut*—

Andrew's right hand closed over her left, resting on the log, half hidden by her skirts.

She snatched it away in sheer shock and pressed against Malena's side, putting another inch between herself and Andrew. Malena, still singing, glanced at her in concern.

"Mosquito," Kate mouthed, and Malena nodded in sympathy.

Andrew sang as though he hadn't even noticed, his gaze on the fire and his hand lying innocently on the log. His leg in its cast was stretched out in front. They moved on to another familiar tune, "Tell Me the Story of Jesus." This time he waited for the third verse before stealthily taking her hand again.

Once more she snatched it away, holding it behind her back so no one would see. She leaned over just enough to hiss in his ear, "Stop it!"

And the rascal took advantage, reaching behind her, capturing her hand again and entwining his fingers through hers as though they'd been dating for weeks. He also had a very firm grip, her hand now trapped in his in the darkness between their two bodies.

"*Neh!*" She tried to keep her voice to a whisper. "Andrew, I mean it. Stop it. Let go."

"*Love in that story so tender,*" he sang, gazing into her eyes as though her own furious emotions weren't obvious. As though he was trying to send her some kind of romantic message. "*Clearer than ever I see…*"

She leaped to her feet and yanked her hand out of his, in her agitation pushing more than pulling. He lost his balance and went over backward off the log, landing with a shout and a clatter as one of his crutches somersaulted over to land on him.

The singing came to a ragged halt as the entire circle stared, the astonished silence punctuated by Andrew's pathetic, "Where's my crutch? Somebody help me up. Kate, what's the matter with you?"

That was the final straw.

The gravel scraped under her sneakers as she ran into the dark. The path up to the house had to be here somewhere. Willows whipped at her face. Here? No, right here, at this break—

She sank up to her thighs in a deep, freezing pool where the river had undercut the bank, and shrieked as she lost her balance. With a splash, she went under, the cold of a river that had had thick inches of ice on it only a month ago spearing through her body, constricting her lungs, snatching away her breath.

Can't breathe. I can't breathe—

And suddenly she was lifted free of it, up into the evening air that felt positively balmy in comparison. Water streamed off her as she felt solid ground under her shoes again. She couldn't see anything, blinded by water and fabric and cold, clammy—

"Get it off me! Get it off!"

Her apron was peeled away from her face. "Kate. Kate, it's all right. Breathe. You're safe now."

Her flailing hands hit shoulders, solid and warm. With one palm, she wiped the streaming water out of her eyes. "Adam," she gasped.

"You fell in. Come on, let's get you over to the fire."

"*Neh!* The house," she panted, gulping in great lungfuls of air. "Can't go back."

"All right. *Kumm mit.* The path is just here."

His arm was around her waist, warm and supportive, guiding her several feet to the right. Her sneakers squashed and slopped as they climbed the shallow slope of the bank through the willows.

On the gravel bar, the singing started up again, ragged and confused, then died out.

"Is she okay?" Rebecca came panting up behind them. "What happened?"

"She fell in the pool under the bank," Adam

said shortly. "It's only four feet deep, but it's cold. I'm taking her up to the house."

"Do you need help?"

"*Neh*, I've got her."

I've got her.

His words, his tone. The sweetest that ever were heard.

Chapter 13

REBECCA WOULDN'T TAKE *neh* for an answer, and in the end, Adam was glad. They slipped in through the back door, where she'd be able to get the shivering Kate into a hot shower before anyone knew what had happened. Adam, meanwhile, retraced his steps back down to the river and settled on the log next to Andrew. The *Youngie* seemed to have given up singing and were talking back and forth, mostly giving Andrew a hard time about everything in life that might be "easy as falling off a log."

As Andrew made room for him, he seemed just as happy not to pretend the teasing was funny. "You all right?" Adam asked casually, stretching his damp legs out toward the flames. "Didn't strain the leg?"

"I don't think so." Andrew did a couple of leg lifts to prove it. "I landed on my shoulder. Almost a full somersault."

"Probably *gut* that you did. Better to roll, *nix*?"

Andrew brightened a little. "You're about the only one here who isn't teasing me about it."

"I'm not in a teasing mood." It astounded him that Andrew hadn't asked about Kate at all. It seemed to prove a point that he hadn't seen before. "Kate was pretty shaken up."

"She should be, after pushing me off this log. I could have broken my shoulder."

"Not about that. About falling in the river."

Andrew stared at him. "She fell in the river?"

"You didn't hear the splash?"

"*Neh*, I was singing. Then Rebecca ran off. I didn't know what was going on."

"She was upset."

"Probably sorry about what she did."

"I think it was more about what *you* did. Mind telling me about that?"

"About what? We held hands. It was nothing. Then she jumped up and pushed me, out of the blue."

"It usually takes more than *nothing* to make a girl run into the dark in a place she doesn't know."

Andrew looked up, as if imploring patience from heaven. "I'm telling you, it was nothing. But maybe where she comes from, a man showing that he likes her is a crime. You sure she's not Schwartzentruber?"

Adam declined to be distracted. "I suppose if a girl didn't want to hold hands with you, it might seem like a crime."

"Oh, I'm pretty sure she wanted to. She could have got up and walked away—I gave her plenty of time. But she stayed right there, waiting for me to make my move."

Had she? Had Adam misread the whole situation?

He couldn't have. Girls didn't jump up and run unless a man did something they really didn't like. Or if they didn't like the man.

"Maybe I'll ask her," he said, half to himself.

"Maybe you should mind your own

business," Andrew said crossly. "You're making a mountain out of a molehill."

"I don't think so. I just saw a girl run into the dark and fall in the river to get away from you. Makes me think you should leave her alone for a while. Stay off the Circle M while she's here."

Andrew stared at him incredulously, fumbling for one of his crutches as though he meant to fend Adam off with it. "Are you serious? What are you, her father?"

"Nope, but you'd better hope this doesn't get back to mine. He won't take too kindly to you frightening a guest in his home so bad she could have drowned."

Andrew levered himself awkwardly to his feet. "Well, you won't have to worry about me coming around to scare your house guests." He looked around for one of his brothers. "Noah," he said more loudly, "Ready to go when you are."

"I'm not," Noah said in surprise. "I'm going up to the house to see what's keeping Rebecca."

"Simeon?"

"All right, hold your horses," his oldest

brother said, pushing himself off his log. "Susan, care for a lift home? Even if three's a crowd?"

"*Denki*, that's very kind of you." Susan smiled up at him in a way that made Zach glance across the fire at Adam. His brows rose.

Adam just shook his head. When he spoke to Susan, he did his best to conceal his relief that her attempts to get Daniel's attention had failed so abjectly. He just hoped Simeon King knew what he was in for.

He watched Andrew crutch away across the gravel bar, and his oldest brother give him a hand on the bank. Andrew had better take him seriously, and stay off the Circle M until Kate was gone.

The party broke up instead of people staying around to sing and visit until the fire died down to ash. He let Josh and Sara do the honors of waving everybody off down the lane, and settled on the log once again, not unhappy to have its warmth and crackle and the rush of the river to himself.

Several minutes later he was debating whether to throw another length of wood on, or let it die down so he could put it out and go to bed, when he heard voices and the crunch of several pairs of feet in the gravel. Flashlights swung back and forth. To his amazement, Noah and Rebecca emerged out of the night ... with Kate. The firelight painted her in a golden glow as she approached, touching the curve of her cheekbone and the folds of her skirts in light. He threw the wood on the flames, and moved over so all four of them could share the same log and contemplate it as it caught.

"I didn't expect you back," he said to Kate as she settled beside him. She now wore a purple dress he hadn't seen before, and while she had removed her soaked *Kapp*, he recognized the *Duchly* as one of his sister's.

"We saw everyone leaving. I wanted to thank you."

"You don't need to. We've all hauled each other out of the river many a time."

"But probably not in the dark, or out of their head with panic."

"Maybe," he allowed. "That bend isn't deep, but the water has to be forty degrees. I'm glad I got there quickly."

"I am, too," Rebecca said from her other side.

"But what I'd like to know is why Andrew fell off the log and you took off."

Kate bowed her head, and in the light of the fire he could see her cheeks flush. "He tried to hold my hand."

Noah glanced at Rebecca, then around her to Kate. "Is that bad?"

"It is when you don't like the person that way," Rebecca informed him. "I didn't like it either, when he tried."

"He did think he was engaged to you," Noah pointed out.

"Is anyone ever going to tell me that story?" Kate said plaintively.

Twenty minutes later, when Rebecca concluded the story, Kate's eyes were wide and one hand had gone to her mouth. "My goodness," she said at last. "*Now* I understand. I'm so glad you two got it all straightened out. As for Andrew—I guess I have the honor of being his rebound girl, don't I?"

Adam blinked at her. "His what now?"

She laughed, but it came out more like a strained chuckle. "She's the one a man might turn to to make himself feel better about losing the one who got away. They say she's always temporary, but I don't know about that. Men marry their rebound girls all the time."

"Now that you mention it, I can see it," Noah said. "Maybe I should clue Andrew in. He's like a ping-pong ball, rebounding from girl after girl. Rebecca was his rebound from that *Englisch* girl with the red car."

"And I'm his rebound from Rebecca," Kate said. "At least, he'd be trying if I hadn't put a stop to it in the most embarrassing way possible. Have I mentioned how glad I am that he won't be going to Denver with us? Is that unkind? Am I a horrible person?"

"No, and no," Rebecca assured her. "I'd feel exactly the same in your place, though there was a time when I thought he hung the moon, and the stars, too."

"Hey," Noah said mildly. "You just didn't know *mei Bruder* very well."

"I didn't know him at all." Rebecca shook her head at herself. "Somewhere out there is a girl who will settle him down, and help him respect himself more. Unfortunately, she doesn't seem to be in the valley at the moment, or we could push him toward her."

"I'd rather have a man who had settled himself down, and had already learned to respect himself because God respects him," Kate said. "Men who still need a woman to do all that repair work for them are exhausting."

"Isn't that the truth," Rebecca said. "I shouldn't wish that fate on some unknown *Maedel*, should I?"

They watched the fire in silence for a while, as though the conversation had taken a serious turn and needed to be absorbed. Adam hoped he was mature enough to be settled within himself before he offered hand and heart to a woman. He had been baptized, and had no plans to be anywhere but here—unless *der Herr* told him different.

Truth be told, he felt a little sorry for Andrew. It was one thing to be gifted by God with good looks and talent. But any Amish person knew that the wrapping on the outside had no value to God if the inside didn't also please Him.

At length, Noah stood. "I should be going.

We have a couple of early mornings ahead if we want to get our carpentry projects far enough along for Andrew to handle them alone."

"I'll walk you up to the buggy."

Noah took Rebecca's hand as though he didn't want to lose even that small connection with her as they strolled across the gravel toward the path up to the house.

"What a difference the right person makes," Kate murmured.

Adam got up and tossed another length of wood on the fire, hoping she would understand the wordless indication that she didn't need to leave quite yet.

"The fire feels *gut*," she said by way of thanks as he settled himself on the log once more. "I suppose it will take a few weeks before summer really comes. Didn't you say in one of your letters that sometimes there was a final snowfall in May, just to remind people that *Gott* was still in charge of the plans of men?"

"I did say that." He leaned his elbows on his knees, his hands lightly clasped between them. "Last year, when it snowed on the first of June."

For the first time, Adam didn't feel that burn

of resentment that he had written those words to Elizabeth, not her, and she had no business quoting them. Now, it felt easier in a strange way, not to have to explain himself all the time. They were like two old friends who had known one another since childhood, referring to events in the past.

"I hope it doesn't do that this year." She shivered.

"You're not cold, are you? Your hair is still wet."

With a smile, she shook her head. "Just playacting. But still, the first of June is tomorrow. Should I be nervous?"

"*Neh, der Herr* is too smart to try that trick two years in a row."

"I hope He waits until after Thursday, then," she joked.

"If you didn't go, though, it could dump six feet on us and it wouldn't matter. We might have to shovel ourselves out, but at least we wouldn't have to shovel the roads to get you to the station."

"Ach, Adam," she said, shaking her head. "Between you and your sisters, I'm almost tempted. But even if it weren't for the Kings spending their money on a portion of my ticket, I'm still needed at home."

"What's your mother going to do when you get married?"

"By then my younger *Schweschdere* will be out of school and able to take over my chores. Or I may not get married. *Gott* might want me to be a Senior Single."

What on earth was that?

She must have read his expression, for she said with a smile, "An *alt Maedel*. The unmarried women who are too old for the doings of the *Youngie*, but not included in the doings of the young marrieds and young mothers."

"Like the Zook brothers here," he said, nodding. "Never see them worrying about finding wives. They seem happy to keep house for themselves and make cheese while they're waiting on God to send someone along."

"It's different for women, I suppose," she said thoughtfully. "My cousin's wife, Emma, found it very hard to be in that place—wanting a home and family of her own, but not having the opportunity. Until Grant discovered that all the time he'd thought he was married, he'd actually been a widower. That took a bit of getting over."

Adam leaned on one elbow to look at her incredulously. "How could he not know he was a widower?"

"His wife ran off with an *Englisch* man. She died in the world not long after, but she couldn't be identified by the *Englisch* police. No driver's license, no fingerprints, *nix*? So no one could tell him."

"Wow." He was silent a moment. "Well, if it's any comfort to you, I don't see you becoming a Senior Single anytime soon."

With a chuckle, she said, *"Denki."* The smile faded from her mouth, leaving him sorry and wishing it would come back. "I'd almost rather be single than put up with the young men who think they can get to Elizabeth through me. There's no humiliation quite like the kind you feel when you've enjoyed a couple of rides home from singing, and even a date for ice cream in town, and have invited him home for dinner … only to realize he's gone through all that so he can be in the same room as Elizabeth.

To get her attention when there aren't any other young men around."

"Ouch." He could almost feel the pain of such a moment. "A man like that can't be much of a man. Didn't he think about your feelings?"

"Apparently not." She sighed. "And in a couple of cases, I thought we were actually having fun getting to know each other."

"A couple of cases?" he said in disbelief. "This has happened more than once?"

"Oh, *ja*. Twice for sure, and with the third I never knew which of us he was really interested in. His family moved to Ohio, and he went with them, so I never found out."

"Fools." He couldn't keep the disgust for these unnamed idiots out of his tone. "They're only good for mucking out manure pits for their rest of their lives, treating you like that. What did Elizabeth have to say about it?"

Kate lifted one shoulder in a shrug. "She just asked if it was over, and when I said yes, she went out with them once or twice. But they never lasted with her, either. Nobody did for more than a couple of months, until Mark Yoder came along." She drew a quick breath and touched his bare arm, where he'd rolled up his damp shirtsleeves. "Adam, I'm sorry. That sounded like—I mean—"

"*Ischt okay.*" The place where her fingers had rested so briefly felt like a cool kiss on his skin. "To her, it didn't last. To me, it did. And now—"

She was silent. Waiting for him to finish. Not poking or prodding, just waiting for him to speak. Or not. It was … restful.

"And now it's over," he said with a kind of wonder. "I don't know how, or why. I was in love with her for two years. How could it be over in just a few days?"

"When the blade comes down, there's blood for a little while, and then it stops."

"Not quite the image I had in mind," he said wryly. "But what I meant was, how can my feelings have any value when they can disappear so quick?"

"Feelings have to be fed, don't you think?" She spoke thoughtfully. "Like any other part of us."

"You said that, in a letter." He remembered it well. "It was the one-year anniversary of the day Elizabeth and I met. I remember being in a panic reading that, worried that she was going to break it off. That I wasn't feeding her feelings enough." He, on the other hand, fed off every stroke of her pen. Well, Kate's pen. "And all that time, you were feeding mine."

She tilted her head and leaned over a little. "Is this the part where I apologize again?"

He had to smile. "*Neh*. I'm just coming to realize that Zach was right. Thanks to those letters, we probably know each other better than most people. I resented it when he said that, but now I can see he was right."

"Our families often are, ain't so?"

"*Ja*. So your mother will really be in a bind if you come back next week instead of this week?"

Her gaze was sober, as if she was trying to figure him out. "I suppose a second week won't inconvenience her any more than the first one."

"It's only really ten days. Not even two weeks."

"And like Malena says, the ticket can be refunded. On the other hand, it means I'm by myself for the entire trip home."

"A small price to pay for the wonderful experience of being in the Siksika." Like a tour guide, he drew an arc with one arm to indicate the whole valley, the corners of his mouth twitching. "What with the new muscles you've discovered riding and enjoying dips in the river and all."

"You paint an attractive picture," she said with mock agreement. "It's hard to resist."

"Then don't," he suggested, shifting from teasing to honesty. "Use Dat's phone to call your mother tomorrow."

"She'd make me promise to leave the same day." Kate made a face. "But if I wrote her a letter, she'd get it about the same time I would have arrived. And by then, there would be no point in demanding that I come back."

"See how easy that was?"

"As easy as sinning," she told him sternly.

He laughed and got up, then offered a hand to pull her to her feet, as a friend would. He let go of her hand just as casually, as though he hadn't even felt the slender strength of her fingers. "I'll just throw a bucket of water on the fire, and we can head up. It's been a long day."

To his surprise, she found the galvanized metal bucket on the rocks and filled it for him.

He took it from her and doused the fire. "It's not likely we'd start a forest fire at this time of year, but Dat gets up in the night. He'd see the glow and march me down here to put it out no matter what time it was."

"Better to take no chances," she agreed.

And when the task was done, it seemed natural to take her hand again to guide her across the gravel bar in the starlit darkness. He'd forgotten to bring a flashlight, but there was enough moon to see by. He had to let her go once they were on the trail. He was no Andrew King.

But still, it was funny that he could feel the warmth of her hand in his all the way up to the house.

Chapter 14

Circle M Ranch
Mountain Home, Montana
June 1

Dear Dad, Mom, Elizabeth, and kids,

This is the first day since I got here that I've had a chance to write. The train trip out was long but uneventful, and for the first part of it a couple of Amish families befriended me. I reached Mountain Home last Thursday and Adam Miller came to get me at the bus station. Elizabeth, he took the news of your engagement as well as could be expected, and speaks of you with kindness.

The ride to the ranch was a revelation of the grandeur of God's work. I've never seen scenery like this before. I'm enclosing a postcard I bought in Libby when I got off the train so you have an idea of it.

The family here were busy with branding this year's calves, which took all of Friday and half of Saturday. They ride what they call cutting horses, which are so well trained it's almost like rider and horse have one brain as they cut, or separate the calves from their mothers, and then let them be together afterward.

We were to the bishop's home for church, which is less than a mile away. Yesterday was spring turnout, where the cattle are driven along the highway for seven miles, then taken up the mountainside to spend the summer grazing and getting fat. My job was to act as a roadblock—or maybe I should say cow block—on the highway to make sure the cattle turned in the right direction. Then we kept them all in one lane (mostly) so traffic could get by on the other side. I learned how to ride just enough to stay on my patient horse's back. She did all the real work. I just stuck on like a burr and hoped she didn't break into a gallop or toss me off.

I've been invited by the family to stay another week. I hope it's all right that I said yes. The Millers are so kind, and there's so much to do that another pair of hands is welcome. Lizzie, you'll be interested to know that one of the twins, Malena, is a very talented quilt designer. She's going to give me some tips so that when I get started on your wedding quilt, it will go together well enough to be both pretty and useful in your new home.

I hope you all are well. I plan to buy a ticket for the train leaving on June 8. I'm sure the days will fly by!

Ever your loving
Kate

KATE SAT BACK at the kitchen table to read over her letter. Who would have thought it was possible to reveal so little after experiencing so much! She felt as though she'd become a different person from the lonely *Maedel* who had boarded the train in Lancaster. And if she were honest with herself, the thought of going home to the same daily routines, the same chores, no prospect of a special friend, and nothing except Elizabeth's wedding to spark her interest … well, it didn't do to be dissatisfied. She would just enjoy every moment of her time here on the Circle M, and treasure the memories when she did have to leave.

"Finished?" Malena sat down at the table with her sketchbook.

"*Ja*. It's hopeless to describe everything I've seen and done since Thursday without writing a book." She paused a moment. "I should just suggest that they read Adam's letters from this time last year."

Malena crinkled up her nose. "Wouldn't that be rubbing salt in the wound?"

Kate considered it. "A little, I suppose, but … Adam's letters are in the past for Elizabeth now.

She may already have burned them." She hoped not. Elizabeth might not value them, but Kate did. Every letter now carried the memory of how she had felt when she read it, and the real-life experiences she was adding now were like illustrations. Even though his letters had not been directed at her, her feelings for Adam had made his words come alive.

She folded the sheet of paper and slid it into the envelope she'd already addressed. Then she set it aside and lifted her chin toward Malena's book. "Have you been sketching?"

"I've been toying with what you told me about the Mariner's Compass your sister wanted for a wedding quilt. Do you think she'd like this?"

She opened the book to the place where the filled pages ended and the blank ones began. The drawing took up one whole page. Kate blinked and leaned in. "Oh, my goodness."

Here were the eight points of the star. Here was the medallion in the center. But where the usual compass-like background might been, triangle points and curves unfolded on two levels to form the shape of a flower like an anemone, opening up behind the star.

"Oh, Malena," she breathed. "I've never seen anything like it."

"I've been noodling on it for a couple of days," she said, color flooding her cheeks. "And it wouldn't be too hard to piece. The flower is a variation on the Storm at Sea, if you've ever made one of those."

"I haven't, but my mother has."

"If you think your sister would like it, I could draw it up properly, with the measurements and the piecing on graph paper. Now that you're going to stay a few more days, I'd have time."

Impulsively, Kate leaned over and hugged her. "I can't think of anything I'd like more than to make a quilt you designed. And I know that Elizabeth will be thrilled."

She was ninety-nine percent certain of that, anyway. Surely Elizabeth wouldn't insist on a copy of the one in Barbara Byler's home once she saw this beautiful original design. Kate would make it in the colors her sister had already chosen, the cool water-and-sky palette that went well with her fair, sunny coloring.

Malena's cheeks were still rosy as she gathered up the sketchbook. "If you want to catch the mail, you should hurry. Cathy usually comes by ten o'clock."

Kate stuck a stamp on the envelope and hurried to put on her sneakers. The quarter mile walk down the lane seemed to stretch out forever, but she made it just in time. As she passed under the crossbar at the gate, the white pickup crested the hill away down at the end of the home paddock, a couple of acres away.

She collected the family's mail from the friendly blond postal carrier, and walked up the lane more slowly, taking in the beauty of the June morning. All along the fence, purple and blue lupines had somehow, while no one was looking, exploded into bloom. They covered the slopes behind the house, too, and cropped up where you wouldn't expect them, at the corners of the barn and at the base of the steps up to the house.

Adam came out of the barn slapping his straw hat on his thigh. Bits of hay showered to the ground, which was already beginning to harden with the warm days. She waited, the mail in her hands, for him to look up and see her.

He smiled. "Hey. Anything there for me?" When she handed over the whole pile, he pulled all the circulars and junk mail out to go in the woodstove, leaving letters, news, and business correspondence. "Here are a couple of things for my brother Daniel. Want to walk over to his place with me, and deliver them?"

"Sure," she said. "I'll just run the rest up to your mother."

When she came back down the steps, a glow of happiness kindled inside her to see him waiting at the bottom.

"*Denki* for fetching it for us," he said.

"I sent my letter home, telling them I was staying until the eighth."

"Just until the eighth?" He cocked an eye at her as he led her past the barn to where a track had been cut through the trees beyond, probably in the last year. It led in a gentle curve around the river meadows in the direction of the house she'd seen from the gravel bar.

"I don't dare stay longer. She won't be happy about my taking advantage of being so far away to tell her what I'm doing, rather than asking."

"But you're of age," he objected. "And a member of the church. That gives you a certain amount of freedom, doesn't it?"

"It does, but I'm still living under my parents' roof. The work keeps three of us busy. I don't want to burden them for very long."

"I suppose you're right. When I went out to Whinburg Township that summer, Dat had to hire an extra hand here. We all knew it would cost, but at the same time, our cousin Melvin Miller needed the help."

"I hope I'll be able to help you all," she said. "Though compared to yesterday, it seems almost sleepy around here this morning."

He nodded. "You wouldn't have said that if you had to check the cows in the barn who aren't feeling well, or adjust the dams in the irrigation ditches so the water keeps flowing. Those chores have to be done every day, no matter what else goes on. Though on church Sundays we let the ditches manage themselves and just check the cows. They don't manage themselves so well."

"Do you have many sick ones?" As they walked, she drew deep breaths of warm, pine-scented air, with notes of earth and grass.

"Not at the moment. One new mother dropped her calf really late and had a hard time because of it. And we have couple of old girls who won't go up the mountain anymore. They're good for teaching the young ones, though, so we keep them healthy and they stay in the home paddock. And Del, my horse, picked up a stone or something in one hoof, so I'm expecting Alden out sometime today."

"I'll be glad to see him," she said. "He was the one acting as *Vorsinger* at the river last night?"

"That's him. He has a nice voice. I hear rumors that Dave and Cal's dad, our *Vorsinger* for church, is going to ask him to lead on Sundays once in a while. Get him some practice."

"Poor Alden." There was a big difference between starting "Country Roads" for your friends with no one but the trout to hear if you made a mistake, and starting the *Loblied* or one of the other slow hymns in front of the entire *Gmay*.

"I suppose it's a bit like choosing the bishop or one of the ministers," Adam said. "*Gott* directs the hymnbook with the long piece of hay into the right man's hands. Maybe He gave Alden his voice because He knew we would need him someday."

"You're right, of course," she said. "I hope he sees it that way, too."

"We're sure glad to have him. He's a *gut* man. His mother moved the family here after they lost their dad to cancer. He'd been apprenticed to his dad and opened the blacksmith shop as soon as he found space. After a year with the local vet to learn to be a farrier, he's got all he needs in his buggy and looks after all the horses in the church, plus a fair number on the *Englisch* ranches."

"Does he help the vet, too?"

"Sometimes. But then, I think you've probably noticed that out here, folks help each other."

"I have noticed that. And you told us about it in your letters, too."

He might have responded, but they crested a little rise, and there was Daniel's house, snug and sturdy and enjoying a view just as stunning as the one from the family home, but from a different angle. The front windows looked over the water meadows and beyond them, the home paddocks, with the highway far in the distance.

In the yard, a small figure whooped and waved, and dashed into the house.

"The word is out," Kate said. "So much for sneaking up on them."

"Nothing gets past Joel," Adam agreed. "For a boy who was afraid to leave his mother's side, he's taken to the Circle M like a goose takes to water."

By the time they reached the yard, Daniel and Lovina had appeared in the doorway to greet them. The scent of something baking was sweet in the air. Kate handed over the mail and then Joel grabbed her hand in one of his, and Adam's in the other. "Come see what we're doing."

"Joel, let them say *guder mariye* at least," Lovina chided him, half laughing.

But all the same, she and Daniel followed

them into the living room, where it was immediately clear what was going on.

"Bookshelves!" Kate exclaimed. "Oh, I've always loved built-in bookshelves. Do you have so many books?"

"No," Daniel admitted. "But what we do have is a barn full of antiques. *Mei Fraa* thinks that if we display the smaller pieces in here, we can hang a sign out at the road for the tourists."

"Oh, *gut* idea," Kate said. "And maybe some folded quilts of Malena's in those longer bays by the windows."

"Exactly. *Quilts and Antiques*. Three words guaranteed to make a woman, at least, turn up the lane." Lovina grinned at her as though they were co-conspirators in getting Malena's wonderful quilts into people's hands.

"I wasn't so sure about tourists tramping through my home," Daniel admitted, "but when Lovina reminded me that some of the pieces Joel's father found are really valuable, I couldn't relegate them to the barn, either."

"There is plenty in the barn," Lovina said. "But these belong in a home setting. Kate, can I show you my wedding quilt?"

"I'd love that."

Leaving the Miller men to talk bookshelf construction, she followed Lovina down a short hallway to the main bedroom, which also looked out on the water meadows. And then she caught sight of the quilt on the bed, and drew a long breath.

"How beautiful." Reverently, she traced the feathers in the borders, and the skeins of pieced triangles like birds heading across the quilt. "Flying Geese?"

"The bishop's wife calls it *Flying Home*. Those borders with the geese in them were Malena's idea. They made it for Daniel and me for a wedding gift."

"It looks so at home here, like it was meant to lie on this bed and no other. Malena and I were just talking about a quilt design for my sister. She'll be married in the autumn and wanted a Mariner's Compass. You should see the beautiful sketch Malena thought up. It's going to take every ounce of skill my mother and I have to do it justice."

Lovina gazed at her, clearly puzzled. "Malena offered one of her designs? Even though your sister is marrying someone else now, and not her brother?"

Kate had not thought of it quite this way. "She's very generous."

"Malena finds joy in the creation." Daniel came up behind his wife and slid his arms around her waist. "She's like the meadowlark. No holding back the song because one set of ears is more deserving than another. The point is to sing. To praise *Gott* with the gift He's bestowed, *nix*?" He kissed the back of her neck just above the neckline of her dress, completely unconcerned that they had witnesses.

"*Ja*, you're right," Lovina said, and turned in his arms to smile into his eyes. "It's a *gut* little lesson for me when I go to sell her quilts."

"If she'll let you," Adam said. "I never saw someone with so much talent so shy about people seeing the things she's made."

"It's a part of you, what you make," Kate said slowly. "Maybe she finds it difficult to expose that side of herself to others."

"Malena?" Adam and Daniel said in simultaneous disbelief, and Kate had to laugh.

"All right, maybe not. You are better judges than I am—I haven't even known her a week."

"Will you stay for some *Kaffee*?" Lovina asked, turning in the direction of the kitchen. "I just took a batch of pecan marmalade muffins out of the oven."

"The day after turnout is always a lazy day," Adam said in response to Kate's inquiring look. "And breakfast was a long time ago. Besides, I'm thinking we should go into town to get you a nonresident fishing license. We'll need sustenance for the journey."

They spent an enjoyable hour with the newlyweds, talking about their plans for their home and property, and reminiscing about mutual friends in Whinburg Township, before Kate became convinced that they ought to let the little family return to their labors.

"Come again, any time," Lovina said, giving her a quick hug. "I've enjoyed getting to know you. I've known your family for a long time, of course, but being in the other church district, we didn't see so much of one another."

"I will," Kate promised. "And … I'm really glad you've found happiness again, Lovina.

There is such contentment in your face, it practically shines out of you."

"*Gott* had quite a job getting me out here and in front of Daniel again," she said, looking up at her husband. "But I'm so glad He didn't give up."

Kate had never seen such love in a man's eyes, except maybe in Reuben's when he looked at Naomi. Or Joshua, when he saw Sara cuddling little Nathan. With a pang, she wondered how happy her own parents' marriage was. Dat was always kind, but he spent most of his time in the barn and shop. They only really saw him at meals.

It felt disloyal when she said something of it to Adam later, when they were driving into town to Yoder's Variety Store, which sold fishing licenses. "And when he and Mamm are together, it isn't like Daniel and Lovina. Like two halves of a whole, designed by God. It's like … a business partnership. With one silent partner."

"They say bringing up *Kinner* is quite a business," Adam quipped.

"You know what I mean. Your parents—the

way they look at each other—still, after six *Kinner*—"

"Seven. Deborah."

"Seven *Kinner* and however many years of marriage. I don't know why I've never thought about it before."

"It helps to have examples," Adam offered. "I didn't see much of your parents when I was there, but I remember thinking your father was a silent man, as you do. Even with the other men in church, he didn't share much. Not that I'm criticizing. A man who can keep his own counsel is less common than I used to think."

"There's keeping your own counsel, and there's not communicating at all," Kate pointed out. "I'm glad you're not like that."

"Still not much of a talker, though."

"But when you do talk, you have something to say. Unlike Andrew King or even David Yoder, who don't apply any thought to their words before they unleash them on an unsuspecting listener."

He chuckled. And then they were turning into the variety store's lot, and there were far to many distractions for speech. Once she had her license in hand, and had resolutely closed her eyes to spending any more time in the aisles, she asked him when he planned to go fishing.

"This afternoon. Mamm was making hints at breakfast about making her special fried trout."

She was delighted not to waste a single day of the license. "Around four o'clock? The sun will be off the water then."

"I'll be ready."

Even with the pleasure of the five-mile ride home, the hours until four o'clock seemed to stretch away forever.

Chapter 15

THE KITCHEN DOOR opened and Naomi glanced up from the letter she was reading, the rest of this morning's mail in a heap in front of her. Feminine voices floated down from Malena's workroom upstairs, where her girls were talking quilts with Kate. Deborah and Nathan were napping, giving Naomi the gift of time to enjoy her letters. Adam stepped in, the breeze from the open door wafting across the kitchen, a bouquet of lupine in his hand. He closed the screen door, as though he knew she enjoyed the scents of the outdoors.

She smiled at the sight of her middle child,

bearing up under a blow that would have knocked anyone sideways, and yet taking the time to do something so sweet and considerate. He seemed to be recovering—more quickly than she had expected. She waggled the letter. "Your Aendi Maysie sends her love. She's expecting again at last."

He got down a vase from the cupboard over the propane fridge, ran water into it, then filled it with the glorious burst of purple and blue. "It must run in the family. Having a long gap between children, I mean."

Maysie was his favorite of her sisters, maybe because she was the youngest. Thirty-odd years ago, their help with a wedding had been the means of bringing herself and Reuben together. Her middle sister, Grace, had moved with her family to the Monte Vista district in Colorado, but Maysie and Amy Jane hadn't gone so far—only to St Ignatius.

He put the vase in the middle of the kitchen table, then swiped an oatmeal chocolate chip cookie.

"*Denki, mei Sohn*. These are beautiful. As for

Maysie, At least she didn't wait twenty years, like me," Naomi said. "Five isn't so bad."

"Do you still want some trout for supper?"

This was so like Adam. Like his father. Hearing her mention something in passing, and then taking it upon himself to get it done for her. "I do. I was hoping someone would take the hint before I had to go down and catch them myself."

He grinned. "You know what Dat says."

"The worst day fishing is better than the best day working."

"I hope it won't be Kate's worst day. We went and got her a license. She likes to fish."

Naomi paused in her happy contemplation of his flowers, and looked up. "Does she, now? Flies or lures?"

"Flies. Do we have a set of waders that will fit her?"

She pictured the poor girl trying to stuff her dress down into the legs. "Adam Miller, no self-respecting Amish girl is going to climb into a pair of rubber waders."

"You used to."

"When it was necessary. To feed my hungry

children, before we got the ranch established the way it is now. You put on waders if you like, but I can guarantee she'll be perfectly happy on the bar."

"That's one thing she never wrote about," he said, munching his cookie and studying the pile of letters on the table. "Fishing."

She could think of a good reason for that. "If she was writing as her sister, and her sister doesn't fish, it probably wouldn't have come up."

He nodded, his gaze still on the mail. "She says that Elizabeth doesn't like camping, either. Things that are messy, in general."

"Then it's a lucky thing *der Herr* doesn't want her to be a Montana rancher's wife," Naomi said with a laugh. "Plenty of ways to get messy out here—though I wouldn't say a Pennsylvania dairy farm is as neat as my grandmother's parlor, either. Plenty of mess wherever there are cows."

His gaze took on a faraway quality, as though something had struck him, the way a hammer might strike one of the metal rails in the corral and make it ring. What had she said?

Der Herr doesn't want her to be a Montana rancher's wife.

"How did I not see that?" he asked, mostly to himself.

She didn't pretend to misunderstand. "I suppose, like many, you were dazzled by a very pretty young woman. And after that, your correspondence was among three, not between two. It muddied the waters. Maybe Kate wasn't willing to paint her sister in an unflattering light. She seems like the kind of woman who thinks the best of others."

"She's let slip a few things," he said. "About Elizabeth not liking to be messy. And how popular she is—was—with the young men. All things that I saw, or would have seen on my own, if I'd stayed out there longer."

"There's probably a few messes Kate would rather avoid, too," Naomi said. "I noticed she gave the boys who were gelding the bull calves a wide berth. Can't say as I blame her. I was always glad to leave that to your father and the hired hands."

"But you would have done it, if Dat needed you."

"Of course."

"She says Elizabeth flat refused to go camping. Maybe that's different. No one thinks camping is necessary. Not like ranch work." After a moment, he sighed. "I guess I shouldn't be dwelling on Elizabeth," he said. "What's done is done, and anyway…" He trailed off, but Naomi had a little idea about what he'd meant to say.

"Kate is here and she's turning out to be not so bad after all." She allowed her voice to quirk up at the end, so it might have been a question or might not.

"You were right about my feeling I know her." He leaned on the counter. "I didn't want to. Figured it would be impossible to tell which parts of those letters were her and which were Elizabeth. But in the end, it seems they were mostly her. The thinking parts, anyway. Not the news parts."

"I wonder if you know how unusual that is." Naomi turned Aendi Maysie's letter over—her funny, thoughtful, newsy letter. "By the time we start having families, most of us don't have much time to think. We certainly don't have time to go into depth about our lives. Just keeping up with the day to day takes nearly everything we've got." She looked up.

"Kate does think about things," he said in answer to that look. "And she talks about them, too."

"Do you answer her? Your thoughts about those same things?"

He nodded. "She's easy to talk to."

Goodness. Maybe she hadn't needed to call in the bishop's wife for help with this little project. Maybe it was happening all by itself. Because *der Herr* had a good eye for a woman who might be happy as a ranch wife.

"I noticed a few of the boys agree with you," she said casually. He could take that any way he liked.

He pushed off the counter, then seemed to change his mind and turned back. "Andrew King won't be around the ranch much. He overstepped and I told him he didn't need to visit until Kate left."

Slowly, she lowered the letter to the table, shocked and doing her best not to show it. "Does your father know?"

"I took care of it."

"This wouldn't have something to do with Kate falling in the river last night, would it?"

"That was after she pushed him off the log. She got disoriented trying to come back to the house. I was right behind her and was able to pull her out of that undercut pool near the path. The water is still cold."

The water was always cold. A person just appreciated it more in August. "The things my children don't tell me."

"You taught us to deal with things ourselves, and if we couldn't, then to tell you. I knew you could help, but it wasn't necessary."

So, Andrew had crossed a line—far enough over it that Kate had had to take drastic action. And instead of sitting back and watching, Adam had chosen to help her.

Naomi watched her son snag another cookie and head outside once more. She returned her gaze to the vase of lupines, sweet messengers with the good news that winter was over and the blessings of summer lay ahead.

For sure and certain, *der Herr* didn't need her

and Sadie's help. He was perfectly capable of making this unexpected match on His own.

ADAM COULDN'T CONCEAL his pleasure when he came out of the barn in a pair of hip waders, with several rods in one hand and a collection of flies stuck in his busted-up straw hat, and saw Kate waiting just outside. She wore sneakers with no socks, no apron, and a *Duchly*, which in his sisters usually meant they were prepared to get wet.

"I was hoping you meant to come," she blurted.

He looked at her, a little puzzled. "Miss a chance to fish? Are you kidding?"

"Well, you might have changed your mind."

"I never change my mind about fishing. *Kumm mit.*"

She lost no time in following him through the gate, then down the path to the river. The first time they'd come down here, when he'd learned she liked to fish, it had ended in pain and recrimination. Now it felt … fun. He'd been looking forward to it.

How strange was the healing hand of God.

"So this is an elk hair caddis," she said, examining the one he handed her.

"We use what we have on hand, same as your father, likely."

"And the fish like to see something familiar," she said, as though repeating something her dad had said when she was a child. "Do the elk come down to this elevation to drink?"

"They sure do. Calving is just getting started, though, so we probably won't see any. The bulls have already headed up into the mountains. But next month, if you keep your eyes open—"

"I won't be here next month." She concentrated on the fly she was tying on the tippet.

Of course she wouldn't. What was the matter with him? "Well, anyway, they bring their calves down to the water at dusk. Sometimes we're lucky enough to see them."

A trout jumped after the hatch of mayflies, the insects lit golden by the lowering sun. "A brownie," she exclaimed. She nodded toward the riffle she'd noticed the first time. "I'll be there. What about you?"

"There's a hole under that cut bank opposite. They ought to be hungry and thinking about coming up."

She found a place where she could keep her footing above the riffle, and cast her line. As he made his way out into the middle of the big bend, he kept an eye on her. Back and forth, back and forth, she made the fly behave as a real one would. Then, light as a bit of cottonwood fluff, she landed the fly and let the current carry it down to the funnel above the riffle, where she suspected the trout were waiting for their dinner.

Nothing took the fly, so she stripped in the line and tried again. Her body upright, feet apart, one hand controlling the rod's rise and fall, the other the slack in the line, the lazy S-curves of filament she made in the air were a thing of beauty. Some people were naturals at fly fishing. He had to work at it, more for the reward of the fish than for any beauty he was aware of.

But now, he was aware of nothing else. This woman. This place. This moment.

She occupied her bit of river as though she were part of it. Calm, quiet. A breeze came up and carried the fly into a bush on the bank, and she only laughed as she went to retrieve it.

"At least it carried it to this side," she called cheerfully. "I'd hate to have hooked you instead of a trout."

"There's still time," he replied. But it was all he could do to focus on his own line. To make himself stop watching her. She was tall, and in company a little awkward. As though she were always trying to make herself smaller, or less noticeable. Maybe that was a natural result of believing that people thought she was in the way—the one blocking the sight line to her sister. She only expanded like a flower when she was with people who appreciated her, like the twins, or Ruby Wengerd. And here, on the river, she really came into her own.

She'd told him that first night that she had feelings for him. That this was why she had continued to write even after Elizabeth had lost interest. He'd been a howling ball of betrayed love and hadn't had it in him to even acknowledge her. All he'd wanted was for her to go away and for Elizabeth to somehow magically appear to take her place.

Shaking his head at himself, Adam cast again. After the way he'd behaved toward Kate, any feelings she might have had for him had probably died of malnutrition. And for the first time, he faced up to what he might have lost.

How many hours had she spent, in her room or the kitchen or some private place on the farm out there in Whinburg Township, writing to him? How many other young men had gone without a date because she'd turned them down, thinking of him? Surely there must have been one or two who had liked her for herself. They couldn't all have been like those sorry fools, trying to get to Elizabeth through her.

What else had she given up for him? He'd probably never know. Had certainly not spared a thought for it until now. He had to be the most unworthy yokel on the face of the earth—unworthy of the feelings of a woman like her.

She cast again, relaxed and sure, and this time something surfaced with a splash, yanking on the line. She played the fish for five or ten minutes, tiring it until she could land it and toss it in the five-gallon bucket they'd used to douse the fire last night. That seemed to be a signal for the other trout in the river, and he had to give up thinking and daydreaming in a hurry if he wanted to keep up. Within thirty minutes or so they had their limit.

"This should be plenty for everyone," he said, wading back to the gravel bar with his last fish. "Eight of us, plus you and Sara."

"Not the hands?"

He shook his head, dispatched his catch, and put it in the bucket with the others. "Dave and Cal go home at night. The *Englisch* hands travel through looking for work, and the same guys show up every year. They stay in the bunkhouse and eat supper on their own, mostly, unless Mamm invites them to eat with us. They stay until after roundup, when the cattle go to auction."

"And they get on all right with the Amish ranchers?"

He had to smile at that. "The ones who don't tend not to come back. With no electricity for

TVs and phone chargers and such, some don't last a day. But there are a few who would never pass up a chance to hire on here when they know they'll be getting Mamm's good cooking."

She laughed as she hooked her fly in the cork handle of the rod and did the same for his. He picked up the bucket and hefted it. Just as if they'd rehearsed it, each took the part of the task for which they were best suited.

"Feeling sweaty in those waders?" she teased as she followed his not-quite-graceful progress through the willows and on to the path.

"Not me. I just got out of forty-degree water. And they're not insulated. I think my legs might be as blue as my pants."

"Ouch," she said. "You really swim in this river?"

"When it's hot. Sometimes, after a long day riding fence in the burning sun, all we can think of is getting our boots off fast enough to jump in, clothes and all. It doesn't feel so cold, then."

"It's a blessing, just waiting for you."

"*Ja*, it is." He smiled over his shoulder at her. "Though you probably didn't think so last night."

"I'm reconsidering," she said. "Can't blame the river, can I? Is it glacier melt?"

"Yep. Bad for people just now, but *gut* for trout. Thanks for giving me the excuse."

She held the cattle gate for him. "Maybe we can go again. I got the five-day license."

It felt like someone pushed him in the stomach, to be reminded that her time here was so short. "Mamm will be thrilled to have trout again."

Zach and Dat met them as they came out of the barn. Zach took the fish and followed Kate up the stairs to the house, while Adam took the rods into the tack room, peeled himself out of the waders, and hung them from their peg to dry.

He was still a little shaken from his realization earlier. The question was, would he do anything with this new knowledge before she left? If she still had feelings for him, would she welcome his admission that he just might be starting to return them?

He'd parked himself on the ancient ladderback chair to put his work boots on, when a sound in the doorway made him look up. Dat leaned on the door frame as though none of the hundred things a rancher had to do before supper held any urgency at all.

He tilted his chin toward the drying waders. "How'd you do?"

"Full limit between us. Mamm will be happy."

"Me, too. I had a hankering for trout this morning."

"No wonder she was dropping hints."

"You had company, too. Not often you see a young Amish woman in the river. Or one with form that good."

"That's a fact." Adam pulled on the other boot. "Becca likes to fish, but she's more about function than form. Catch the fish, eat the fish. Straightforward."

"Looks like Kate's about both. Nice of you to take her down there, if she enjoys it. You getting on better?"

Adam felt the heat burn into his face, and got up to adjust the rods in their cabinet before he put the box of flies on the shelf and closed the tall door. "It's a little easier, I guess."

"Not still holding it against her that she's not her sister?"

Trust Dat to come right out and say it. "It wasn't that. I felt deceived, is all. Stupid, for thinking I was having this big love affair. I was, I guess. I just didn't know I was in it by myself."

"Not quite by yourself, from what I hear."

Of course his parents had been talking. There was no point in trying to swerve around the issue, not when it practically camped out beside him every minute.

"Kate told me she had feelings for me. That's why she went along with it."

"Mm." His father rubbed at something on the floor with the toe of his boot. "And now?"

He lifted a shoulder. "After the way I treated her, I wouldn't blame her if she changed her mind. Took up with Dave Yoder instead. He's interested. At least Andrew King is off the list."

"I heard about that from your brother earlier. You did right. But what about you, son?"

"Well, that's the thing." Adam leaned one shoulder on the tall cabinet door and contemplated the floor. It needed sweeping. "What business do I have with any sort of feelings? I'd be as shallow as that river down there if I took notice of somebody else so soon after getting my heart broke. What kind of man would that make me?"

His father thought this over. "The kind that learns, I guess. You're like that with horses, too. Get bucked off and climb right back on again."

"Kate's no horse."

"Never said she was. I was talking about you. And your ability to learn lessons when they're given."

"Love isn't a lesson."

Dat chuckled as though he knew different. "Maybe not, but it can sure teach a man a lot about himself. God's love has that built right into it. But between a man and a woman, it's harder. Is Kate different here from when you knew her in Whinburg Township?"

Adam did his best to work his way toward the truth. His father deserved that, and anyway, Dat was in the habit of truthfulness with his *Kinner*. "To be honest, I didn't really see her. Stand her up beside Elizabeth and you don't even know she's there."

"Must be hard for a *Maedel* to live with that. It would be hard for anyone."

"So I'm learning. There's a man or two I'd like to dunk in a freezing creek for courting her, just so they could use her to get close to her sister."

"I'd help you carry them to the water." His father gazed at him. "She seems to have come into her own here, though."

"*Ja.* It's like I'd never met her before I saw her at the bus station—I didn't even recognize her. Don't you think it's strange that I could know her so well through her letters and yet I walked right past her? She had to *introduce* herself, Dat."

"It is strange, yep."

"And then she learned to ride just so she could go with us for turnout, and stuck on Marigold's back even though she was afraid. And then to find out she and Lovina know each other—to see my sister-in-law be more friendly and welcoming than I was—well, there was a lesson. And she hasn't held any of that against me. Just been herself, like you say. Enjoying herself with us."

"Probably enjoying a bit of sun on her face, instead of standing in her sister's shadow."

Maybe that was the crux of it. "That, too."

"Must be quite a shadow. I don't recall any of you having that kind of trouble among yourselves."

"An Amish person doesn't go around looking to stand in the sun. Elizabeth doesn't. At least, I never noticed it."

"Maybe because at the time, you thought she *was* the sun."

He absorbed his father's words. He was being awfully generous with the truth today. "Maybe I did. I was blinded by it."

"That happens when we look into the sun. The natural kind or the human kind. We forget it's the Son we're supposed to see in each other."

He had to admit that the light of heaven had not been the first thing on his mind when he'd first laid eyes on Elizabeth. But there was more to it than that. Everything he'd realized over the last couple of days—everything his father had said just now—gelled into a conviction.

He rubbed his eyes with one hand. "I made an idol of her, didn't I." It wasn't a question.

"Don't be too hard on yourself." A warm hand came down on his shoulder and squeezed. "A person can be dazzled by another human being just as surely as the sun dazzles when it bounces off the river. It's what you do after your vision clears that matters. When you can see properly again."

The sight of Kate standing on the gravel bar, casting with such grace, came into his memory, every detail as real as life.

Elizabeth, he already knew, had been the dream.

"What am I going to do?" he muttered, half to himself.

"Seeing her properly is a good start," his father allowed. "Let her see you that way, too."

It was *gut* advice. He cocked an eye at Dat. *"Denki."*

"Neither of us are much for talk." Dat crossed the little room and paused in the doorway. "But I'm always here if you need me."

"I know." And for that, Adam knew he would be thanking the *gut Gott* tonight in his prayers.

Chapter 16

AS A CHILD, Kate had been able to feel the moment when winter got tired of being cranky and cold, and finally gave in to the life and warmth of spring. And in giving in, changed everything for the better.

Adam, it seemed, had decided that being cranky and cold was no way to live. Instead, he was becoming more like the man he had been in his letters. Warm, thoughtful, and with the occasional crack where he let his sense of humor shine through.

Three days had passed since the two of them had gone fishing. While his and his brothers' days were filled with ranch work and he and Sara had one call-out with the volunteer fire department, she looked forward to the evenings, when they were all together. Then, not only was her body satisfied with a good meal she had helped to make, but her soul was satisfied simply by having him near. Holding his baby sister so that Naomi could work a little on the tiny sweater she was knitting for her. Listening to Daniel and Lovina talking about the newest skill Joel had mastered in his quest to be a rancher like his stepfather. Patiently giving his opinions about color choices to Malena as she held swatches of fabric together in various combinations.

The pattern for Elizabeth's Mariner's Compass wedding quilt was completed and folded carefully into Kate's suitcase. There was so much math in the drawings that Kate's whole spirit heaved a sigh of relief that Malena had figured it all out, so that Kate didn't have to. All she had to do was take the paper pieces and cut them out, put them together according to the instructions, and there it would be, ready for quilting, backing, and binding some six months from now.

When Adam overheard her talking with Rebecca about Lucy Maud Montgomery's *Anne of Green Gables* books, and how much she'd enjoyed them as a child, he'd taken the trouble to hunt out his mother's collection for her. Along with the old favorites, he unearthed some titles she'd never read—*Jane of Lantern Hill* with its young heroine attempting to reunite her parents. *Anne of the Island* and her choice between two men—and two dreams. *Pat of Silver Bush* and the danger of loving one's home too much. And the one that became her favorite, *The Blue Castle*. There was something about its plain little heroine being transformed by love, to the point that even her beautiful cousin had to grudgingly admit it, that appealed to something deep inside Kate.

On Saturday afternoon, she had been looking forward to curling up on the sofa with *The Blue Castle*. But when she looked out the front window and saw Adam swing a small rucksack up on his shoulder and look up at the house, she drew a breath, hardly daring to hope.

It could just mean that he had a repair job to do somewhere. Some ditch dam or chunk of fence that needed the tools sticking out the top of the canvas sack. But when Adam took the steps two at a time up to the door, she could hardly breathe for the anticipation that backed up in her chest.

He took her in at a glance. "Dat wants me to check on the pump up on the ridge behind Mammi's orchard. Do you feel like a walk?"

"Does it involve cows?" she asked, only half joking. There wasn't much around the Circle M that didn't.

"Only indirectly. The pump keeps the water running into the tank and the ditches, which makes the hay grow, which feeds them in the winter."

"Good enough. I'll just get my sneakers on."

He'd put two bottles of water in the pockets on either side of the pack—another little piece of evidence to add to the growing pile that told her how considerate he was. As they passed the home paddock, Marigold came to the fence as though she, too, wanted to come along.

"Magic for Marigold," she murmured as they walked up the path behind the house.

He glanced over his shoulder. "What's that?"

"It's the title of one of the Montgomery books you brought me. Marigold is the name of the heroine."

"What's magic about her?"

"I don't know—I haven't got to it yet. But if the twins read it, I wonder if the mare you lent me was named after her."

"Who knows where the twins get their ideas?" His tone was half indulgent, with a smile in the other half.

"Have I told you how much I'm enjoying your mother's books? I never knew most of them existed. It's like a treasure trove."

"I'm glad you like them. I think I even read some of them, years ago. Wasn't there one about a girl who was a writer?"

"Emily of New Moon," she said. "Three of them. The last one was kind of awful, though. When she grows up and finds out the man she thought she loved burned her manuscript."

"I didn't like him from the start. Too self-centered."

"Exactly. Willing to destroy the thing she loved because it took her attention away from him."

"Plenty of folks out there like that." Ahead, the path forked, and he pointed to the right. "That way is Mammi's orchard. Maybe we'll stop in on the way back. Or maybe you've already seen it."

"*Neh*, not yet. Why do you call it that?"

He guided her toward a steeper path that wound past an outcrop of granite and then widened so that they could walk side by side.

"Mammi Miller planted a bunch of apple trees in there. Everyone thought they'd die in their first winter, but something about that canyon makes them happy. It's watered and sheltered just enough that they're able to grow."

With a smile, she said, "The whole ranch is like that. For people."

"I've thought that a time or two, as well." He returned her smile and her heart did a somersault in her chest. "The growing season here is only about three months. The soil doesn't support crops the way it does in Whinburg Township. That's why most families don't farm. We ranch, or provide services like Alden Stolzfus, or open a shop, like Lovina wants to."

Kate looked down at the roof of the house, far below. "We've come a long way in ten minutes, haven't we? No wonder I'm out of breath."

"Sorry." He stopped and stretched his back under the pack. "It's pretty steep. But look over there." The ridge ran west to east, and just below them, on the south side, was a small meadow, filled to the brim with lupines.

"Look at them—blooming for all they're worth while they can," she said. "They just seemed to spring up between one day and the next."

"They're Mamm's favorite flower. Malena likes the wild roses, and Rebecca watches for the glacier lilies in spring."

"And you know their favorite flowers?" Honestly, what man could say the same? Except maybe his dad.

He shrugged, and something in the pack clanked. "Seems to me you said in a letter that your favorite was the bearded iris. But now I'm not sure if you meant your own, or if you were telling me Elizabeth's."

She had to laugh at herself. "No, that was definitely Lizzie's. My favorite is Queen Anne's Lace. Not quite so showy, but I like the way dozens of individual flowers make up a big one. All lacy and delicate, yet able to stand up to the weather."

"A bit like God's people, then," he said. "Lots of individuals, separately kind of ordinary and small, but together they make something beautiful that can stand up to the world."

"Now, see?" She turned from the view to show him she was ready to walk on. "This is why I loved your letters. They sound just like you."

Was it her imagination, or was there a flush of color in his cheeks? She supposed a man wouldn't like that pointed out. Still, it was one of the things about this walk that she appreciated the most. Along with the smell of pine pitch warming in the sun, the alpine flowers peeking out from behind clumps of granite or thriving near a shallow spring, the animals that only allowed a glimpse before they were gone—eagles, deer, squirrels, some of the ranch's cattle, and higher up, even a bobcat.

"Don't see those often," Adam said in a low tone as the creature vanished into the trees. "They're shy. In some ways. Mamm keeps our chickens secure, just in case they and the coyotes get up the nerve to visit."

"Do you shoot them?"

He shook his head and continued up the slope. "This is their habitat. We keep the calves and chickens safe, but other than that we share the land with them. Good husbandry doesn't mean killing off predators, because that only causes other problems, like the deer overgrazing the pastures."

The higher they climbed, the more the view opened out. And the more Kate realized the extent and the grandeur of the mountains around them.

"Here we are." Adam swung the pack off his shoulder and she saw a small shed in the clearing with a windmill to power it. "I won't be long."

"Need some help?" From beneath the shed

she could hear the gurgle of water—another natural spring.

He grinned. "I hope not. If I do, it means I've got a bigger problem than I expected."

She sat on a flat rock in the sun while he cleaned out whatever was stopping the pump from doing its job. And evidently it wasn't much of a problem, because in twenty minutes he was putting the tools back in his pack and pushing the shed door closed with his hip.

"That's that taken care of. Until the next one gets silted up."

"How many do you have?" They walked through the meadow the way they had come, knee deep in grass. In the pines, a calf bawled at them as if it resented its treatment by the cowboys yet.

"Just four, plus the main line that goes into the house and the barn. Dat put them in when he became a partner with his father in the ranch. Back then, gravity fed irrigation was pretty newfangled."

"Your family moved up here in 1974, I think you said."

"Good memory. So you can figure how old

Mammi's orchard is. Come on. It won't take long to get there. Going down is always easier than going up."

For which she was grateful. Going for a walk here in the Siksika wasn't a bit like walking in rolling, open Pennsylvania, with its long-established roads, rich fields of corn and soybeans and tobacco, and its thick copses of oaks and firs.

Adam dropped his pack at the mouth of a box canyon and led the way in along a path fringed with rocks, grass, and the red flowers of Indian paintbrush and yellow daisies similar to the brown-eyed Susans that grew at home. The canyon widened out and there they were—six trees with gnarled branches, thickly leafed out now that blossoming season was past.

"My goodness, I never would have expected to see this," she exclaimed. "How many varieties did she plant?"

"Only the kind that handles the weather best." He touched one as though it was an old friend. "Here in northwestern Montana, that's a Lodi. Mamm makes the best schnitz pie you ever tasted from these apples."

One more thing she'd miss out on, she thought with a pang, once she got on that train.

He must have noticed her silence, because he leaned on a trunk. She stopped, too, and idly peeked under a cluster of leaves to see the tiny apples that had set. Apples that would go in a pie sometime in October. What were the chances Adam would savor that pie, and remember standing here with her?

"I owe you an apology," he said.

She looked up in surprise. "What for? The walk was steep, but it wasn't so bad."

"Not about that. About the way I behaved when you first got here."

It took her a second to jump over the gap between expectation and reality. "I don't blame you for it. I did an awful thing—and arriving to wallop you over the head with it on no notice at all didn't help."

"Maybe so, but I know I upset you. Grieved you. I hope you'll forgive me for it."

"Of course I do, Adam. I did days ago. You had much more to forgive, believe me." She lifted her head to meet his gaze. "And I'm glad you did. It seems … easier between us now."

He nodded, as though he thought so, too. "I wanted to be sure it wasn't just me feeling easier. If we're going to be friends, I didn't want that beginning standing in the way."

Going to be friends. Hearing those words on his tongue was like tasting the sweetest apple that ever grew. And yet … there was a slight edge of sourness in them, too. Because she did not feel like a friend. It was all she could do to keep the love in her heart hidden—in check— under control. Not when it wanted to burst into bloom and wrap itself around him. Wanted to express itself in words that didn't have to be examined and toned down before she spoke them.

He was waiting for her to say something.

"Are we?" she asked. "Going to be friends?"

"I feel as though we already are."

"I do, too. Funny what a difference it makes when I can speak for myself instead of always sifting what I say through what Elizabeth would say. Like flour through a sifter." She smiled up at him. As a friend would. She hoped that nothing more showed in her face as she joked, "Was it *gut* or bad that

I had to think twice before I wrote anything to you?"

"Most people would say it was *gut*, but in this case I'm glad you put the sifter away."

She still had to sift her words through her feelings. But at least both were her own.

His gaze lay warm on her face, as though it were sunlight. Or maybe it was her face that was warm under it. Ach, was she blushing?

The truth was, she'd never really had a man's undivided attention before. It was a powerful thing. Maybe she should move. Break the connection. Go back to the house, where there were people and activity and not this breezy, expectant silence. She didn't want him to think she wanted more than he was willing to give.

"Adam—"

"Kate—" he said at the same time. Then he chuckled. "Go ahead."

"I forgot what I was going to say." Which was a tiny fib. She just couldn't say what she wanted to.

"Then let me ask you something. I want to be not just friends, but *gut* friends."

That wasn't a question. But she'd answer it

anyway. "I do, too. It's nice to spend time like this, just talking about whatever comes to mind. Like *gut* friends do."

"It's almost like starting over. Like the letters and your sister and all that never happened."

But this didn't feel right. "*Neh*, I don't think we can just put a cover over the last two years and pretend they aren't there," she said slowly. "I didn't go through what I did on that train trip for nothing, and you've been through a lot since I got here, too. We paid a price to come out on this side. Our friendship wasn't free."

He gazed at her, and she could swear she saw appreciation in his eyes. "That gives it value, then, doesn't it?"

She nodded. "I think so." Did she dare say more? Her insides felt shivery at the prospect of letting out just a little of what she felt. "I value it."

"Your friendship means a lot to me, too. It's … special."

A jolt ran through her, as though the air were charged with lightning. Did he mean *special* as in one of a kind? Or *special friend* as in two people who were courting?

Ach, neh, that couldn't be. Adam simply wasn't the kind of man who could absorb the betrayal he'd experienced last week and then transfer those feelings to someone else, just like that. Not Adam—loving, loyal Adam. Maybe a year from now he would be able to contemplate a life free of loving Elizabeth. But in a week? Impossible.

"Kate?"

"I—I'm—I don't—" She took a step back and felt the thick branch of the apple tree just below her shoulder blades, like the supporting arm of a friend. With a deep breath, she said, "It's funny, isn't it? How different a special friendship is from being special friends. Same words, almost. But they mean completely different things."

"They don't have to." His brown eyes were steady, a smile lingering on his lips.

Now the branch pressed against her back, preventing her from turning away. So she had to say it to his face. "I don't understand. Don't play games with me, Adam. Speak plainly."

The smile fell from his mouth. "I didn't

think I was. I thought I was leading up to this gently."

"Leading up to what?" She didn't know whether to shake him or kiss him or duck past him and run away.

"The question I wanted to ask you. What do you think of our being special friends, Kate?"

The hurricane of emotion whirling inside her went silent with shock. Her mouth opened, but not a single word came out.

"I know it's crazy." Color climbed in his tanned cheeks. "You probably think I'm shallow. I think I must be, feeling like I did for Elizabeth and now feeling the opposite. Like she was a dream and you're the real thing. But—" He stepped closer, his boots nearly touching her sneakers in the grass. "What I don't know is how you feel."

"She can't be a dream," she finally got out. "You didn't write to a dream for all that time."

"I think I did," he said, as though finally realizing it himself. "I finally figured out … it wasn't her letters I was waiting for. It was yours."

"But—"

"I know. It's a tangle. But we've untangled ourselves now. We can speak plainly to each other. And I have to say that I was never like this with Elizabeth."

"Like what?" She hardly knew what she was saying. How could she, when he was offering her dearest dream in his big callused hands?

"Easy together." He chuckled. "Working together. Fishing together. Who does that with his special friend? But maybe we do. Maybe we do things differently from other people."

And maybe this was completely impossible. "But Adam … I don't want to be your rebound girl."

The warmth faded from his eyes. "You're not."

"You say that, but how can it be otherwise? I read your feelings for my sister in your letters. Feelings like that don't just die overnight and get reborn for someone else."

"Maybe they weren't the kind that last. Maybe something that begins with friendship has a better chance."

"Or maybe you need to give yourself a chance. To recover. To get over her."

"You don't think I'm over her?"

"I don't think hearts work like that. You were angry at first. Maybe now it's time to grieve. And in time, to accept it truly. And only then to move on."

"You've got my feelings all mapped out for me."

"What are friends for?" she quipped, but he was having none of it.

"How long is this process supposed to take? A month? A year?"

Oh dear. She'd annoyed him now. "I don't know. I guess everyone is different."

"I agree with you there. Well, let's see how different we can get."

And before she could even take her next breath, he'd slid an arm around her waist and pulled her to him. His lips came down on hers—hard at first, then when she opened her mouth to make a noise of protest, he softened the kiss. His mouth became persuasive. Tempting.

She mustn't give in, she couldn't … but oh my goodness, this was how she'd always dreamed of being kissed. Every furtive peck in a darkened buggy vanished into insignificance, burned away by the reality of Adam.

When he finally released her, both of them were gasping for air. Both of them had taken, and given. And in doing so, she had felt the edge of desperation in the heat of his body. Desperation to erase Elizabeth through her.

And that decided her.

"We shouldn't have done that," she said breathlessly.

"But we liked it."

"That doesn't make it right."

"Kate, listen to yourself. Of course it's right. I'm free. You're free. What is stopping us?"

She brushed bits of bark off the back of her dress and straightened her *Duchly*. "I meant it. I'm not going to be your rebound girl. We can write as each other if that's what you want. But only as friends. Not as … anything else."

She turned and made her way through the apple trees. There would be fruit at summer's end, but not now. Now there was only leaves and possibility.

He followed her out of the canyon's shelter, snatching up his rucksack on the way past.

"That's what you want? More letters? When are we going to get to know each other in person?"

"We have a week. And a five-day fishing license," she said over her shoulder, navigating the path down to the house. It was fairly wide, but tricky with rocks and switchback turns.

"But what about after that, when you're home in Pennsylvania?"

It was not lost on her that they seemed to be going backward, not forward. But she couldn't see any other way. "We should ask *der Herr* to show us His plan."

"And you want me to be satisfied with that?"

The answer was so obvious that she didn't bother to say it aloud. If *Gott* planned their lives a certain way, then of course any Amish child of His should be satisfied.

At the steps that led down into Naomi's kitchen garden, he turned aside for the path that would take him down to the barn.

The kitchen door opened and Naomi stepped out, looking as though she'd just put out a fire in the kitchen. Or something just as bad.

"Adam?" she called, her tone sharp with urgency.

He corrected his course and joined Kate on the stairs, following her down. *"Was ischt, Mamm?"*

"You just got a call on the fire phone."

In an instant, he became all business. "I'll get my gear. Is Sara called out, too?"

"No, it's not an emergency. Not an *Englisch* one, at least," she corrected herself.

"Amish, then? Did Aendi Annie hurt herself?"

"*Neh*, nothing like that. It's—you've—she—" Naomi stopped herself with an effort and took a deep breath.

Kate felt an icicle of foreboding slide down her back.

Naomi's gaze met hers. "She called from the bus station in Mountain Home. It's your sister, Kate. It's Elizabeth. She wants to know how soon someone can come pick her up."

Chapter 17

THY WILL BE DONE *on earth as it is in Heaven.*

The words ran through Adam's mind, repeating over and over as Hester's hooves clopped out the rhythm. *Thy will be done. Thy will be done.*

Beside him, Kate sat in silence, but he could feel her tension growing as the distance to town shrank. There was no point in speculating about what calamity could have brought Elizabeth all the way across the country. They would find out soon enough, and have five miles to hear all about it. To let the shock of whatever it was wear off.

What his family would have to say about this second unlooked-for arrival was another matter for speculation, but at least he could count on one thing. Malena would have an opinion, and she'd waste no time in sharing it.

The bus had gone, leaving the parking lot just as empty as on the day Kate had arrived. He tied Hester to the rail in the buggy shed and he and Kate approached the station. The bench where he had half expected to find Elizabeth waiting was empty.

"She must be inside." They were the first words Kate had spoken since they'd left.

But she wasn't. Even the ticket booth had closed, now that the last bus of the day had gone through. Kate went into the ladies' room and a torrent of *Deitsch* ensued, echoing off the tiled walls so that he couldn't make out a word.

The door was wrenched open and there she was, tears running down her face. Her beauty was like a shock to the system. How could he have forgotten the effect it had on a man?

"Adam!" She flung herself at him, and he barely got his arms up in time to fold them around her. She sobbed against his chest. "I'm so glad to see you—oh, it's been so awful—I thought I'd never get here."

Kate came out behind her, folding toilet paper into usable lengths for nose blowing. Wordlessly, she handed Elizabeth one, and the latter mopped her eyes before using it on her nose.

"Come on," Adam said. "You can tell us all about it on the way home. Where's your bag?"

"Oh—I forgot it inside. I was so surprised to see Kate—"

Wordlessly, Kate went into the restroom and retrieved it. And somehow, when they climbed into the buggy, she wound up on the back bench with the rolling suitcase while Elizabeth took the front seat next to him.

While he guided Hester onto the road, Kate said, "Lizzie, is everything all right at home?"

"Oh, *ja*, everyone is fine. That is, everyone but me." Her voice clogged.

Kate handed her another length of tissue. "What happened? We couldn't think what would have brought you all the way out here if it wasn't something horrible and serious."

"It is horrible and serious!" Elizabeth wailed. "Mark and I broke up!"

Adam glanced over his shoulder to see Kate's face a mask of astonishment, and turning white. He probably looked the same. But this made no sense at all. He was on the point of asking for an explanation, when Kate seemed to recover herself.

"Lizzie, people lock themselves in their room and cry when they have a breakup. They don't spend three days on a train. What on earth …?"

"It's hard to understand." Elizabeth blew her nose. "If you haven't been engaged or even in a long-term relationship."

"Hey, now," Adam began.

"Well, it is."

"I've seen people go through it before," Kate said steadily, as though Elizabeth were simply telling the truth. Her truth.

"How can anyone understand what it means to have your whole life taken away from you, just like that?"

Adam understood it all too well. It didn't

seem to occur to Elizabeth that she herself had been responsible for the experience.

"Did Mark give a reason for calling it off?" Kate asked.

"What makes you think he called it off?"

"Because you love him," Kate said gently. "You were so happy. I can't imagine you telling him you didn't want to marry him after all."

"It was awful," Elizabeth said, burying her nose in the tissue. "But that's exactly what I did tell him." She turned away from Kate in order to speak to Adam beside her. "We had a terrible fight. The things he said to me! I was miserable then, but I've had three days to think about it. To relive it a hundred times. And now I see what a mistake it would have been to marry him. I had no idea he had such a temper."

"He didn't … do anything, did he?" Adam asked, a note of dread sounding deep inside him.

"Other than shout? *Neh.* We were walking by Willow Creek. Making plans. And then it all went wrong. He's lucky I didn't lose my own temper and push him in."

"But what could possibly have gone wrong?"

Kate asked again, wisely phrasing it differently this time.

"That's none of your business, Kate Weaver," Elizabeth said, straightening her skirts and sitting straighter. "It's between me and Adam."

Kate was stricken silent.

So was Adam. Just like that time he had emerged from the pines while riding fence, and come practically face to face with a black bear. He recognized that moment of complete stillness while disbelief fought with panic.

As though the subject had been put in a box and she'd turned the key, Elizabeth said, "Is it far to the ranch?" They had left Mountain Home behind them and were out in open grazing and hay country now.

"Five miles from town," he said, when Kate didn't answer.

"I hope your family doesn't mind having two Weaver sisters land on them unexpectedly."

"*Neh*," was all he could say. "I expect you'll bunk with Kate. There are two beds in the guest room."

She chatted on, asking questions and not seeming to mind that his answers were less than expansive. Did she not remember that he had answered the same questions already in his letters, as he'd described his life on the ranch? Kate had told him that Elizabeth sometimes didn't read them, or simply glanced through them to get to the parts where he told her of his hopes and dreams for the future, or how much he missed her. But what that actually meant was borne in on him now, in a way he couldn't avoid.

She hadn't been interested a year ago. Or even a month ago. Why was she interested in his life now? Was she just making conversation?

"What are those tall blue and purple flowers?"

"Those are lupines. They like high altitudes."

"You remember, Lizzie," Kate said, finding her voice. "One of his letters had a sketch of a lupine, painted in watercolors so you'd know what they looked like."

"Zach is a bit of an artist," Adam managed. "He did it for me on the letter paper."

"Oh, I remember now," Elizabeth said. "He's your brother closest in age, ain't so? I thought that was a delphinium."

Adam had written around the sketch, telling her about a meadow he'd discovered where the flowers had made a carpet of blue, more vivid and intense even than the sky.

Had he ever felt this uncomfortable? What had happened to the pair they had been two summers ago, when it seemed to him he had found his soul mate—and he'd believed she felt the same? Now, he only felt relief when he saw the first of the Circle M fences. Relief, and a need to take Kate somewhere private, where he could ask her if she was all right.

Before long, he said, "Here we are," and Hester turned into the lane without waiting for guidance from him. "Welcome to the Circle M."

"Is that what that means?" She pointed up to the crossbar with their brand carved into it as they passed under it. "M for Miller."

"Mm-hm."

"And the circle?"

"Depends on who you talk to. Mamm says God's will. Daadi used to say it meant the valley."

"What do you say?" She smiled up at him. The smile that used to empty his mind of everything except how to get her to smile at him like that again.

"I think it stands for the family circle."

"I like that," Kate said behind him.

"I was just going to say so, too," Elizabeth said with a nod of agreement. "What a pretty place."

"As pretty as hard work can make it. But more than that, it's useful. These fields and paddocks keep the cattle safe. Those ones closest to the barn are for the horses."

"But these are mostly empty," Elizabeth objected. "I thought you said you had hundreds of cattle."

"They're up on the mountainsides now," Kate said. "Spring turnout was last weekend, when the family and a bunch of neighbors helped drive them up to the allotment."

"My goodness." Elizabeth turned with raised eyebrows. "I bet that was exciting."

"It was. I got to help. Malena and Rebecca taught me how to ride just well enough to be a roadblock on the highway." Kate chuckled.

"You learned to ride?" Elizabeth sounded

astonished. "Astride? Better not let Dat hear about that."

"Things are different out here," Adam told her. "Every pair of hands is needed. Like a roadblock at the gates on each end of the drive so the cows don't wind up all over the valley—or worse, under a diesel rig."

Any more conversation had to wait, for here was the whole family outside in the yard. Someone had clearly been watching for them. Adam climbed down from the buggy and made the introductions while Kate took her sister's suitcase into the house. His father took Hester into the barn, leaving Adam free to go with his guests into the house.

"You must be hungry," Mamm said, ushering Elizabeth up the stairs and into the kitchen. "Help yourself to anything you like. It's almost coffee time anyway—let me get you some."

Mamm and the twins and Sara had loaded the table with all the good things they had on hand, and before long, the whole family was in the kitchen, asking questions about her trip and was she exhausted and would she like to hold a *Boppli*? Elizabeth took Nathan on her lap and cooed to him while she savored a piece of raisin pie with cream poured over it, trying to eat and keep his fingers out of it at the same time.

She was *gut* with a *Boppli*, he could see that. But then so was Kate. Amish girls grew up looking after the younger ones in the family, and were comfortable with caring for other people's *Kinner*. Elizabeth was no exception. She appeared to be completely unaware that Zach couldn't stop staring at her. Josh snuck glances when he thought Adam wasn't looking. Even his parents gazed at her as though she were a rainbow or a particularly vivid sunset—some natural event that might not ever come again.

He could not for the life of him figure out why she had come now.

All right, she and her fiancé had broken off their engagement. He could understand heartbreak and disappointment. It was natural for a girl to want the comfort of her sister at a time like this. But to come all the way across the country when her mother and other members of her family were right there? Wouldn't they have done all they could to ease her feelings and support her?

Why was she here? And why had she said that the reason for the breakup was between her and him?

He wasn't sure he wanted to find out.

So, he smiled and spoke and had a piece of pie and some coffee, and then quietly faded out the back door to head for the barn. He needed some time alone. This whole day had been topsy-turvy and filled with emotions that were almost too much to handle. Hearing Kate say *not yet*. Kissing her. And realizing that Kate was the woman he wanted to kiss for the rest of his life.

Oh, he'd kissed Elizabeth, that summer two years ago. It had been almost a sacred experience, coming that close to that perfect face, those stunning eyes. Realizing she wanted to kiss him, too. Daring to press his lips to her soft mouth.

But there had been only the one kiss. And compared to the fire of the kiss he'd shared with Kate ... well, there *was* no comparison. He'd been shaken to his soul, and when he'd opened his eyes to look into hers, to see if it had affected her the same way, he was not the man he'd been when he'd walked into the orchard. Because in those eyes he could see that she felt the same. And it scared her at the same time as it filled her with joy. Just like him.

But she was cautious, and he couldn't blame her. He had to be free of the past before they could contemplate a future. He could see that now, though at the time, under the branches of the apple tree, he'd been frustrated and said things he shouldn't have. He needed to talk to her, to reassure her that he understood, and agreed that they should take it slowly. Maybe he'd ask Dat if he could spend the summer in Whinburg Township this year. In fact, maybe he could go back with her on Thursday if—

"Adam?"

The vision of sitting in the observation car and experiencing the trip with Kate at his side shattered into a hundred sparkling pieces. He came back to himself, sitting on the dusty chair in the tackroom, a length of harness in his hands. He looked up.

"Am I interrupting?" Elizabeth stepped into the tackroom. Behind her, a beam of sunlight fell across the floor from the door and illuminated the space of the barn, giving her an ethereal glow. Her dress was a peach color, her cape and apron black, and even though it was supposed to be modest, somehow the slenderness of her waist was only accentuated by the crossed and pinned apron ties. Her heart-shaped Lancaster County *Kapp* was so starched and clean he wondered how she could have kept it that way if she'd slept sitting up for three nights.

"I was just thinking about giving this harness some saddle soap." But he made no move to fetch it and a rag. "Do you want to sit down?"

She looked around, and he got up in case she wanted his chair. "Could we go for a walk? I thought we might talk a little."

"All right." He hung up the harness he hadn't touched and led the way along the stalls to the sliding door at the rear of the barn. This led into the home paddock, and the gate that opened to the path to the river.

She followed him, taking in the grass, the horses, and beyond them the great granite ramparts of the mountains with the snowfields that never melted on their peaks. He didn't take her down to the gravel bar, but instead along the path Mamm and Dat often enjoyed, winding beside the curves of the banks to a little overlook. Here, Dat had built Mamm a bench out of a chunk of a fallen tree trunk, so that they could sit together.

He couldn't remember if he'd told Elizabeth about the bench. Kate would probably remember.

"This is nice." She seated herself, arranging her skirts neatly, and after a moment, he lowered himself beside her, not touching them. She'd never been the kind of girl you wanted to muss up on purpose. "Who made the bench? Your father?"

"*Ja*, when he and Mamm were first married. They walk out here quite often in the evening to watch the sunset."

She smiled, and gave him the sidelong glance through her lashes that had once made his heart practically leap out of his chest. "It's a romantic spot, then."

"Mamm thinks so." He and Zach had caught them kissing here once, and it had embarrassed their two sons—they'd been ten—so much it had taken him and Zach a year to venture along the path again.

"I think you chose it on purpose." The smile widened. "That relieves me, Adam. I've been so *verhuddelt,* so upset, that all I want is to sit here with you and take in this beautiful view."

"It's a tonic, all right," he said, leaning back against the sturdy slats. "Good for the spirit."

"But more than that, knowing you're here with me." She gazed upward at the peaks. "I've made a terrible mistake. This is all my fault."

"What is?"

She shook her head and returned her gaze to the river. "Letting you go. Getting involved with Mark. Half the attraction was the farm, you know. Of course we're supposed to live for the treasures of heaven, but you can't deny that a partnership in a successful, well-managed farm with that many acres is something you're going to consider when a man asks you to marry him."

"I suppose," he said. "I'm surprised you let him go. Seems like that life would suit you."

"But there's more to life than acres. I mean, you have acres here."

"Not quite a million-dollar operation."

When she glanced at him in surprise, he said, "We do have relatives in Whinburg, if you recall. They've mentioned it."

"It's the truth, as far as that goes. But I want more. I want love." She turned to him, her knee touching his leg. "I want *you*, Adam."

"Before or after the fight with Mark?"

She didn't seem to notice his tone. "Oh, before, for sure and certain. In fact, that's what brought on the whole terrible shouting match. I barely mentioned your name. But it proved to me that I couldn't live with a jealous man. Imagine that being thrown in my face every time we disagreed. I couldn't stand it."

"But I don't understand, Elizabeth. We weren't a thing when you and Mark started courting." At least, she hadn't thought so. He had, but he was kind enough not to remind her.

"But we were still writing, you see." She made a face that combined regret and guilt. "The next day, he came over and made me show him your letters. They were dated well after he and I started courting."

"Mark Yoder read my letters?" Adam sat up. "Those were private."

"They weren't that private if Kate read them."

"That's not the same. She wrote the replies. Which, I might just point out, I thought were from you."

"Oh—" She flapped a hand, as though his words were mayflies rising around her. "I'm not good at letter writing."

"You deceived me."

Her eyes widened. "Kate was the one carrying on. I hardly had anything to do with it, except as a friend."

"Then why did Mark get so upset, if they were just the letters of a friend?"

"They weren't. You know that. Not once Kate got going. And Mark wouldn't take my word that it was really her writing to you. Because of course there weren't any of *her* letters in that shoebox. They were all yours."

Evidence of his love for the woman he thought he was writing to. Had actually been writing to.

"What a mess," he said, half to himself.

"But it's not a mess now." She laid a hand on his arm. "Everything is clear. I read those letters properly, Adam, once my engagement was broken. And they were beautiful. True expressions of love. I can hardly believe you feel that way about me."

You'd have known if you'd read them. He bit back the words. Because it didn't matter now. Those letters had been written to a dream girl. She was still a dream girl—there was something not quite real about Elizabeth Weaver. Not quite present in the here and now of a life with mud and cows and snow and sunsets so beautiful they erased everything from the mind but praise of the Creator.

"Adam, I'm going to be completely honest with you." The warmth of her hand had penetrated his cotton shirt sleeve. "I've never stopped caring. Never, even when I got my head turned by Mark Yoder. Can we put all that behind us and start again? Because I don't want to be his wife. I know that now. I want to be yours."

Chapter 18

ADAM WAS GOING to go back to her.

Kate knew it beyond a shadow of a doubt—after all, who had ever been able to resist Elizabeth? Even as little scholars, she'd seen both boys and girls fall to Lizzie's charm and beauty, and it had only become more of a reality as the two of them got older. One or two of the boys hadn't even waited until she was sixteen before they had the boldness to ask if they could walk out with her. The only thing that chased them off was Dat, who was less bothered by the attempt than he was at the inconvenience of having to wait up for his daughter's return afterward.

She finished helping the Miller women put away the remains of the pie and cookies set out to welcome Elizabeth. There had been no such welcome for her, she reflected, but then again, she wasn't the one Adam loved. Though there had been that glowing moment when she thought she might be ... there in the orchard. When he'd kissed her.

And then, as though *Gott* had chosen that same hour to make His will known, the fire phone had rung and she'd realized that all her dreams were just that. Dreams.

She had been his rebound girl. Now that his first choice had come for him, there was no point in pretending anything different.

Naomi glanced at her. "The twins have gone. Aren't you going with them?"

There was something comforting about Naomi—for every confidence her *Kinner* shared with her, she likely had an experience in her life to relate that would help them work through their troubles. But Kate very much doubted she'd had an experience like this.

She glanced around the empty kitchen, at

the damp cloth with which she'd been aimlessly wiping down the counters. She hung it over the stove rail. "*Neh*. Maybe I could help you make supper?"

"It's already in the oven. A roast, with potatoes and onions and carrots. All I need to do later is make a bean salad."

Now that she mentioned it, Kate could smell the roast cooking.

"Your sister and Adam have gone along the river walk," Naomi said. "Past the gravel bar where you were the other day. At the end of it there's a lookout. Reuben built a bench there for me, because the view is just staggering and he knows I love it."

A *gut* place for a reunion.

"It's even better now," Naomi went on. "Daniel and Lovina's house is snuggled down into that view. Makes it even more special to me."

Kate made a sound in her throat that could have been agreement. Or maybe despair.

"Maybe you could tell me why your sister is here?" Naomi leaned a hip on the counter as though she meant to stay awhile. "No one wanted to bring it up over coffee, but probably everyone but the *Bopplin* wanted to know."

There was no reason not to tell Naomi. After all, this was her home and they'd both landed on her without warning. She deserved an explanation.

"She broke up with the man she was to marry."

Naomi's brows rose. "The one with the partnership in his dad's big farming operation?"

"Mark Yoder. *Ja*."

"But why?"

Kate lifted a shoulder. "I don't know. But I expect that's what she and Adam are talking about down there. She said it had to do with him."

"Ah." Naomi tilted her head. "This other man found out the letters were still coming, even after she promised to be his wife?"

"I don't know," Kate said again. But it made sense that this would have caused a problem.

"Ach, poor Adam," his mother sighed. "And now here she is, probably looking to warm up cold soup."

Kate felt as though she had just walked into

a door. Naomi had just spoken aloud the very idea Kate had just had in the privacy of her own mind. Or more accurately, that the soup had never gone cold to begin with. "Maybe."

"Would she do something like that?"

"I feel as though I hardly know her anymore," she confessed. "I think all the attention she gets has gone to her head. If she can't have Mark, maybe she's come to the man she can have."

"Just so she can feel like she hasn't been rejected. *Dumped* was the word we used when I was young. It's an ugly word, I always thought."

"It is."

"But it's not a very good basis for a relationship, you have to admit."

"They seemed to have a pretty good relationship before." Kate had seen it playing out, practically firsthand. Maybe it was the pain at being the one he hadn't chosen that seemed to etch those memories deeper.

Maybe that was why she'd been so eager to fall in with Lizzie's plea to write her letters for her. It hadn't been a favor to her sister at all. It had been so she could maintain the fragile thread of connection with Adam Miller. Turning every word she'd written to him into both the truth from her heart—and a lie.

"But the point of writing letters is to deepen a relationship," Naomi said. "To get to know the other person. And the result, from what I've seen, is that he knows you far better than he knows your sister."

"That may be true, but it may not matter now." Her throat closed up and her eyes filled with tears. She blinked them back, but it was already too late.

"Have faith, Kate," Naomi said gently. "Faith in *Gott*'s will, and faith in *mei Sohn*."

As well as his mother might know him, she didn't know Kate. Didn't have a lifetime of experience in being second choice, if she was chosen at all. Kate was nothing if not a realist.

So she smiled weakly and went away upstairs to the room she was going to share with her sister. Closed the door. And wept, as quietly as she could, for the death of the hope that had dared to bloom in her heart, as bravely as ever any apple blossom dared to bloom in the face of a raw Montana spring.

WHY DID he keep remembering that day in the alpine meadow? The black bear had looked up and seen Adam astride Del. The instinct of the prey, he knew, was to remain motionless and wait for a distraction that would take the predator's attention off it for just one second. And in that second, it would flee.

Del hadn't waited even for that. He had wheeled and galloped into the pines, nearly unseating Adam. It was only by the grace of *Gott* that it hadn't been early spring. If it had, the bear would have been bad-tempered and hungry, and far more likely to give chase.

Now, here he sat beside the Siksika River, with no distraction in sight, and no Del to carry him away to safety. No one from his family would come down here. Not when they thought he was having a romantic moment with the girl of his dreams.

Maybe he ought to pray for that bear.

"Adam?" came her soft voice. "Tell me what you're thinking."

"About bears," he blurted.

She blinked, and removed her hand from his arm. "I tell you I still care, and you're thinking about bears?"

He scrambled for something sensible to say. "It's late in the day. Sometimes they come down here to drink." Like every couple of years, maybe. "We should keep an eye out."

"And if I asked your mother, would she say she watches for bears when she's sitting in this romantic place with your father?"

"She might. We don't come with them unless they want us to."

She tapped his arm playfully. "I think you're trying to distract me. Isn't that just like a man? But this is too important. Adam, truly, I need to know if you feel the same way."

"You spent three days on a train to come and ask me that?"

"Kate did," she pointed out. "Did you talk about bears when she got here?"

"No. She broke the news to me in the buggy on the way home. That you were engaged to Mark. That she had been writing your letters for at least a year and a half." He turned toward her. "Be honest, Elizabeth. What kept you writing? Why didn't you just tell me?"

"It wasn't me writing, as you just said."

"Then why didn't you stop Kate?"

She gave him her shoulder under the pretense of looking at another angle of the view. "I don't know."

He could only see three-quarters of her face, but it was enough. "Was it because you like having two men on the string?"

She folded her arms and looked away. "Of course not. What an awful thing to say."

"If it's not true, then I apologize. But you can see how it looks from my point of view."

"Then your point of view is wrong. I thought we were friends. Anyone can write to their friends, whether they're male or female."

"But we're Amish," he said. "When an Amish man and a woman agree to write, it means more than that. It means that, while they might be separated, they want to build the relationship. Make it more. I thought that's what I was doing."

She was silent, studying the river.

"What I didn't know was that you didn't read most of them. Or at least, only pieces."

"If Kate told you that, she's lying!"

What a thing to accuse her sister of! "I don't think she was. Because all the way home this afternoon, you asked questions that told me you hadn't read them. I told you all those things before, in my letters."

"I remembered the flowers—the lupines."

"You did," he allowed. "But not that I told you about a meadow full of them, and how I felt when I discovered it."

"I can't remember *everything*, Adam."

"But if you'd really cared about my life here, and maybe even the possibility of sharing it, you might have remembered some things."

She bounced around to look at him again, and captured the hand lying on his knee. "But it's the possibility of sharing your life that brought me all the way out here. Oh, let's forget the mistakes we made in the past, and think about the future. You do care, Adam. I know you do. You have since the moment we met."

"I did," he confessed. And took a breath, like someone who was about to jump in a stream he knew was only forty degrees. "But I don't feel the same way now."

She stared at him as though this thought had never occurred to her, even once, during all the miles she'd traveled to have this conversation. Then her disbelieving gaze changed as something struck her.

"It's Kate, isn't it?" she said on a note of discovery. "She tried to take you away from me, and she nearly succeeded, didn't she?"

"She didn't try to do anything. And besides, with your engagement to Mark, I believed I was free. Why shouldn't we be friends?"

"Friends? Or something more?"

"I'm not going to talk about Kate behind her back."

"Then there is something there," she said triumphantly. "If you were only friends you'd talk about her the way you talk about anybody. The people here. Your family. Your horses."

Del was the closest an animal could get to

being a friend, but he still didn't appreciate Kate being compared to him by her own sister.

But she didn't see his frown. She had jumped up. "I'm going to settle this once and for all."

And before he could stop her, she took off down the path at a run, her loose white *Kapp* strings fluttering out behind her.

Chapter 19

"WHERE'S KATE?" Elizabeth's voice came up the stairwell from the kitchen, followed by Naomi's softer reply, then by the thump of feet on the stairs. In a couple of seconds, she pushed open the bedroom door and closed it firmly behind her. "Here you are."

Kate sat up, fully aware of the tracks of tears on her face. With the hem of her apron, she scrubbed them away.

"I knew it. Only one thing would make you cry, and that's me being special friends again with Adam."

"Are you?" she managed. Her stomach turned over with dread.

"I asked him point blank, and he didn't say no."

He was probably still in shock at seeing her at all.

"But he was very clear about what you've been up to with me out of the way." Her sister folded her arms on her chest. "I'm waiting."

Kate gathered up her self esteem and her wits, and patted the beautiful quilt that covered the bed. "Sit down, Lizzie."

"I won't. Not until you answer me."

Kate pushed herself up against the headboard, the comfortable pillow at her back. "All right. First, you were engaged to someone else. Second, he was free. Third, there was no *getting up to* anything." Well, except that moment in the orchard that was so precious she would never share it with anyone. Especially not Elizabeth.

"Then why are you blushing?" her sister said triumphantly.

"Because it's embarrassing that I have to have this conversation at all. Two people were both free to become friends. There is no sin or underhanded business here. And once we got the whole letter-writing mess straightened out, he forgave me. So I was able to forgive myself."

"If you're looking for *my* forgiveness, Kate Weaver, you'll wait a long time."

It was difficult to figure out what she needed to be forgiven for, but asking would only lead to an argument. "That's between you and *Gott*."

"No, it isn't," her sister snapped. "It's between you and me. And what you've been doing."

Kate gazed at her, unable to help the pleat of confusion forming between her brows. "Did you not hear what I just said?"

"I heard a lecture. But there have been so many over the years they all sound the same."

Is that what Elizabeth really thought of all their sisterly talks? That they were only lectures? Somehow, in all this mess, a needle of pain found its way to her heart. "I'm sorry for it. I don't mean for any of our conversations to be a lecture."

"Well, most of them were." Sounding slightly mollified, Elizabeth plunked down on the bed.

"Especially when you start counting on your fingers."

"I don't—" Oh. "Oh, dear." Her lips twitched.

Lizzie shot her a glance over her shoulder.

But she couldn't help it. She laughed. "You're right. I do that, don't I?"

"More often than you know."

She nudged her sister's hip with one stockinged foot. "Sorry. I'll try to do better. Or at least do the counting behind my back."

But Lizzie, for all her many gifts from *Gott*, had not been blessed with a sense of humor. She would simply look like this, mystified and annoyed, while her sisters went off into gales of laughter about something silly.

"So where does this leave us?" Kate asked gently.

"I want you to promise to stay away from Adam."

Kate's lungs constricted, and while she was trying to take a breath, Elizabeth went on, "It's not fair for you to distract him when he really cares for me. He's just hurt, and like any man, is trying not to show it."

Breathe. "If he cares for you, nothing I can do will distract him."

"He has to work through the pain of my engagement, still. And now that I know he still cares, I know that he's worth waiting for."

Did he care? Still?

> So often I look to the left when I go down to the mailbox. In the pines, just up the slope, there's a flat spot perfect for a house. It wouldn't be as large as my parents', but it would be big enough for us, our Kinner, and to host church of a Sunday. It wouldn't be filled with much in the way of furniture just at the beginning, but it would be full to the rafters with love. I can see it now—the sun shining through the kitchen windows in the morning, turning your hair to gold.

Oh, why did she have to remember that now? It just proved what Elizabeth believed. A man who could write those words probably did still care.

"All right," she said. Her voice didn't sound like her own. Hollow. Empty. Making a promise her heart didn't want to keep. "I'll book a seat on the train as soon as possible. I was supposed to go home Thursday and I haven't booked it yet. Maybe this was why."

"And leave me here?"

Kate stared at her. She didn't understand the question. "*Ja*, of course."

Elizabeth shook her head. "Book us both tickets for Thursday. I'm not traveling across the whole country by myself twice in one week."

"But … why would you go home at all? Don't you want to stay here with Adam, and get to know his life firsthand?"

"Who says I have to live here? Maybe he'd rather move to Whinburg Township and start a new life there."

"That's not what his letters said."

"Which you would know, of course."

"Which you would know, if you'd read them. Seriously, Lizzie, his whole heart is here in Montana. You can't just expect him to uproot himself from everything he's ever known."

"He would expect *me* to do that. *Whither thou goest, I will go. Thy people shall be my people, and thy God my God.* Isn't that what's embroidered on the sampler at home in the living room? Mamm's wedding sampler?"

"Because it's the woman's place to go where her husband wants to settle, not the other way around."

"It's supposed to be a joint decision," Elizabeth informed her in the tone of one who had been engaged to someone who had not. "Besides, it would be much easier to find work at home than here."

Did she not know Adam at all? "He has work here. He's a partner in the ranch. All the boys are, except Joshua. His fiancée has a hay farm already, and he's going to build a shop there this summer. He's apprenticing to be a saddle and harness maker."

"Riding around all day chasing cows isn't work," Elizabeth said, dismissing Joshua. "I mean something that brings in a paycheck, like a regular shift at the RV factory, or building buggies for our people in a buggy shop."

"Adam would suffocate in either of those jobs," Kate said a little flatly.

"Oh, and you know so much about him."

"*Neh*, but I do know that."

"Love can work miracles." Lizzie stood and went to the bedroom door. "I meant it, Kate. You're just friends. You've said so yourself. Mind you keep it that way."

It was the hardest promise she'd ever been asked to keep. But for Adam—for him to have the woman he believed *Gott* had chosen for his wife—she would agree.

All the same, she couldn't say the words *I promise*. So she simply nodded, and Elizabeth left the room with a step as light as air.

———

THE NEXT DAY was the church district's off Sunday, for which Kate was thankful. Having to share a room with Elizabeth was normal, even on the other side of the country. But Kate couldn't sleep, and even though her sister was exhausted and dropped off right away, every movement, every sound just served to remind her that tomorrow, she would have to avoid Adam.

With shadows under her eyes, and a pale

face, she made a poor contrast with Elizabeth as they gathered with the family in the sitting room after breakfast. Having had a full eight hours—Kate had counted every one—Elizabeth looked radiant. Even with her head bowed, listening to Reuben read from Scripture, she was the picture of glowing, modest femininity.

All right, then. Kate couldn't compete, so she wouldn't. Staying out of his way would be easy.

The old Bible went around the room, each person reading as many verses as they chose—even little Joel, who took it as seriously as if he knew he might find the long straw in a hymnbook some day.

> Leah was tender eyed; but Rachel was
> beautiful and well favoured. And
> Jacob loved Rachel; and said, I will serve thee
> seven years for Rachel thy younger daughter.
> And Laban said, It is better that I give her to
> thee, than that I should give her to
> another man: abide with me. And
> Jacob served seven years for Rachel; and they
> seemed unto him but a few days, for the love
> he had to her.

Surely Reuben hadn't chosen these verses on purpose, Kate thought in despair. But no, it was just *der Herr*, gently reminding her that the younger sister was beautiful and well favored, and of course Adam would do anything Elizabeth asked of him.

Even move away from Montana, if that was *Gott's wille*.

Kate lasted through lunch, and then when Naomi invited her to go with the family over to the King place to see how Aendi Annie was getting on, and so Rebecca could hear any news of Noah and Simeon's arrival in Colorado that she didn't already know, Kate simply couldn't face it.

"I don't feel well," she said in a voice that was a wisp of its former self. "I'd like to just rest quietly in my room, if that's all right."

Naomi laid a warm hand on her forehead. "No fever, at least. But you do look peaky. You do what you think best, Kate. We should be home around four. Reuben likes to make sure the stock are tended to well before dark."

She had promised to stay out of Adam's way, and she was keeping her promise.

It felt every bit as wrong now as it had done yesterday.

———

SIMEON AND NOAH KING had gone to Colorado to wind up their affairs there, rent out the house they'd built to a family who had been corresponding with them since the spring, and complete the construction contracts they'd already signed. Adam watched with a smile as Rebecca drank in every word of the family's latest news, as if each task completed meant Noah would come back to her sooner. He liked Noah's family—his parents and two sisters, at least. He still had a few lingering reservations about Andrew.

Andrew had shown them around the farmhouse, with its renovations both completed and in progress, as though he had been personally responsible for bringing new life to Aendi Annie's original family home. Was it her recent approach to the marriage vows that had Elizabeth so interested in things like insulation and new plumbing? Or was it simply that she and Andrew had hit it off almost at once—after that first moment when Andrew got his first glimpse of her climbing out of the buggy? Adam was quite familiar with the effect she had on men—the jaw drop, the stillness as they took her in, as if struck by a bolt from the blue.

He had felt exactly that way, once.

But no longer.

Like an indulgent brother, he watched as the poor *Narr* made a fool of himself over her, directing his remarks to her, angling to make her laugh. Adam had done the same, two years ago. It was enough to make him shake his head at his past self, to see it all repeated. And when Andrew crutched upstairs with Naomi and Reuben to show them the finished, furnished rooms, Elizabeth tagged along as though seeing that he made it safely to the second floor was her entire purpose in visiting.

Adam felt nothing more than a sense of relief at finally having the opportunity to slip outside and have a look at the barn, in case the Kings might need more help out there at some point during the summer. They'd already hosted a productive work frolic for the house, but every property in the valley needed a clean, organized barn for their animals, even if all it housed was the buggy horses and chickens. Animals appreciated tidiness as much as humans did.

Rebecca slipped in behind him through the big sliding doors of the bank barn. "I saw you go out. Figured I'd find you in here."

"Think they'll need a work frolic later?" Hands on hips, he surveyed the dusty space. "The structure seems sound. Just needs a *gut* cleaning."

"They might," Rebecca said. "But that's not why you're out here. Adam, tell me … does it hurt you to see her with Andrew?"

He glanced at his perceptive sister in surprise. "About as much as seeing her with Andrew hurts *you*, I guess."

"Which is not at all."

"There's your answer."

She was silent for a moment, absorbing this. "Can I tell you something?" When he nodded, she came closer and boosted herself up on the rail of the nearest calving pen. "Yesterday, when Malena and I were in the workroom, we heard her and Kate talking. Behind closed doors."

"The walls aren't as thin as that, Becca."

"They are when voices are raised even a little." She hesitated. "Maybe it's not my place to stick my spoon in and stir your soup."

"Since it's not being warmed up, feel free."

Rebecca's caution seemed to vanish. "Elizabeth told Kate point blank to stay away from you. That she believes you still care, and that you told her so."

With a clutch in his heart, he ran over his recollection of that memorable conversation. "I don't think I did."

"Well, whether you did or not, that's what Kate believes now. At least, it looks that way if her face this morning was any indication."

"If she got any sleep at all, I'd be surprised," he agreed. "But I thought it was just from having to share a room with her sister."

"I think it's from having to share a lot more than that."

He needed to figure this out. How to tell Kate that Elizabeth had overstepped. How to ask her if that kiss in the orchard had meant anything at all. How to open his heart to her. But he couldn't say all that to Rebecca. This was between himself and Kate.

But Rebecca wasn't finished. "Speaking of sharing, I'd like to know how her being so forward with Andrew works into your being a couple again, in her mind." She glanced at him. "It's not my place to criticize, but I am quite an authority on Andrew and his ability to attract female attention."

"Both of them have that ability. They should get together, shouldn't they? With all the looks and charm, it seems obvious they should be attracting each other."

"Truer words were never spoken," she said with a laugh. "Is she trying to make you jealous?"

He might have made a joke out of it, but for the first time, he realized what he was really seeing. "I think I just figured something out."

"What their *Kinner* would have to deal with?"

"Ha ha. About Elizabeth. This isn't the first time I've seen her do this. It just took me longer to see it because now it's my turn."

Rebecca made a *go on* motion with one hand.

"We were talking the other night about Andrew and his rebound girls. Well, no one would ever call Elizabeth a rebound girl—she's the one every man in Whinburg Township wants. But what if I'm her … let's call it her backup man."

"Her backup man?"

"Elizabeth Weaver always seems to hold onto her old boyfriends. She kept Lorne Beiler, her boyfriend before me, just interested enough to keep him hanging around even after she and I were openly dating. And then she kept writing to me even when she was dating Mark Yoder."

"More than that. Engaged to him."

He nodded, his gaze on the bright sunshine falling in through the open barn door. "So I, obedient guy that I am, have been doing what backup men do. When number one falls out of the lineup, number two catches her and makes her feel better, until he either becomes number one again or a new number one appears."

"Which seems to have happened, right on schedule." Rebecca, her eyes full of sympathy and realization, studied him. "She might have a harder time keeping you hanging around than poor Lorne Beiler. Maybe that's why she told Kate hands off. To keep that option open."

He pushed off the rail and lifted her down. Then he gave her a one-armed squeeze as they strolled toward the door. "If anybody asks, tell them I decided to step out of line."

"The backup man line?"

"Yep. I'm going to walk home. And see if I can talk to the person who thinks I'm the only man in line. I hope she still does, anyway."

"Kate thinks you're the only man on the *planet*."

He hoped Rebecca was right. But her confident tone put wings on his boots as he headed off across the meadows and fields to the Circle M.

KATE HAD MANAGED ONLY a half hour's nap, but at least it refreshed her. It also left her restless and unable to settle to the usual Sunday afternoon activities, like letter writing or reading another of L.M. Montgomery's novels or working on a jigsaw puzzle. The babies had gone with their parents, of course, so she couldn't even play with one of them.

She decided to take a walk.

Not down by the river. And certainly not up to the orchard. But maybe she could find the place Adam had mentioned in his letters, where he had dreamed of building his house. Maybe, she thought wryly, she could torture herself just a little more with the might-have-beens. In any case, it would be a pleasant walk full of birdsong instead of a silent house full of her own regrets.

The sun fell warm on her shoulders as she set off down the lane, her fingers occasionally brushing the nodding spires of the lupines on the grassy edges of the narrow gravel track. She spied a deer trail winding off to the left into the pines and followed its faint outlines, feeling the ground rise toward the ridge that extended behind the family home. When she emerged into a meadow below a big granite outcrop, she saw at once that this must be the place.

A flat spot perfect for a house, he'd written. She wandered through the meadow, thigh-deep in lupines and daisies and waving grasses, entertaining herself with the ways the house might be laid out. If the windows of the sitting room, where church would be held, were to face the river, as certainly they must, then they would come to about, say, here. She paced off about forty feet. The kitchen should face the Miller family home, so that as they cooked and ate, they could see each other's lights twinkling in the distance. There would be a bedroom downstairs, and at least four upstairs, as well as a bathroom on both floors and probably some kind of workroom somewhere. If Lovina was going to sell quilts as well as antiques, there was no reason she couldn't sell the quilts made by the *Fraa* of this house, too.

She could practically see the house rising around her, but she still couldn't decide where to put the workroom.

Which was why she nearly jumped out of her skin when a voice exclaimed, "Kate? What are you doing here?"

She whirled in a flurry of green skirts to see Adam come out of a copse of aspens and walk down a path from the ridge that looked fairly well used. Her heart beat fast—both with surprise and from the sound of his voice. The imaginary house had vanished with a snap, leaving her in the middle of a meadow watching him take a few rapid steps down the last bit of scree between two rocks taller than he was.

She couldn't very well tell him what she'd been doing, so she scrambled for something else. "I thought you went to Kings'."

"I did. And then I walked home."

"You walked three miles because …?"

But he only smiled. "It's not so far when you know whose gates are unlocked and where the shortcuts are." He joined her, hands on hips. "I love this place."

"You described it once, in a letter. I was rambling around enjoying the lupines and thought I'd climb up here. I wondered if this was where you planned to build your house."

"*Ja*, this is it. Dat and I have skated around the idea of this lot being deeded over to me in theory, but even though he and Mamm would love it if we all raised our families on the Circle M, I know he won't talk brass tacks until he sees me stand up in front of the bishop in wedding clothes."

"Mm." She strolled away a few steps and admired the beauty of a particularly tall spire of lupine. "Well, you shouldn't have much trouble there. Though I hope you talk it over with Elizabeth. She's pretty set on the idea of living in Whinburg Township."

"She's free to do that if she wants. Her choices won't affect me."

Kate looked up, confused. "What?"

"She and Andrew seem like the perfect couple, don't you think? Both good-looking, both the middle kid. Both completely convinced that what they want is what everyone else should want for them. Seems like a good match, ain't so?"

In spite of herself, Kate had to laugh. It was the perfect description of both of them. "Did I miss something by staying home?"

"It was like a gasoline fire. You had to stand back to watch or get your eyebrows singed off."

"*Mei Schweschder?* And Andrew King? Seriously?"

"Seriously. Rebecca and I think that two

people with that much in the way of good looks had better stay together, for the good of the community. Keep the fire contained, I guess you could say."

"Rebecca is no slouch on the subject of Andrew."

"That's what she says. And I realized something about Elizabeth." He gazed at her, his brown eyes turning solemn under the brim of his straw hat. "Will it hurt you if I talk about it?"

"Oh, I know Elizabeth pretty well. Much as I love her, there's not too much left that would surprise me."

"Well, I came to a few conclusions. It isn't that she likes more than one man on her string. What she likes is to keep a backup man."

Kate could only nod, understanding at once. "Lorne Beiler and you. You and Mark Yoder. Now you and Andrew, maybe. I don't know why she does this, Adam. She can only marry one of you."

"And I'm nobody's backup man, always available when something goes wrong. Just like you're nobody's rebound girl, standing around waiting to catch them. I want to be someone's one and only. And face whatever goes wrong and whatever goes well with that person."

Kate's knees nearly went weak at the rush of longing that swept through her. What wouldn't she give to be that woman! Because he was certainly that to her. Why had she told him she wouldn't be his rebound girl, that he had to wait a year to get over Elizabeth? She must have been *batzich*.

And he had gone to Elizabeth because she'd asked him to … seen the truth … and come back.

Why had he come back?

The trembling in her legs moved on to the core of her, and out to her hands. She was shaking like the aspens in the copse above them.

"I know you said you wanted me to wait," he said as though plucking her very thoughts out of the air. "But Kate, I still believe, right from my heart, that you are that person for me. The one and only. Am I that for you?"

"You know you are," she whispered. "You have been for two years."

"Is that why you're standing in the sewing room in my house?"

She looked down at the meadow flowers. "This is the kitchen." She pointed in the direction of the highway, concealed by pines, and made up her mind. "The sewing room is there, so you can see customers coming up the lane to Lovina's shop, and see the sunset as well. There's a bedroom there, too."

"Oh, I see." Laughter danced in his eyes as he swung in the other direction. "Next you'll be telling me the kitchen is here because it has to look out toward the lights of Mamm and Dat's house as well as Daniel and Lovina's."

"Well, it does. And so they can see the lights here. Each family will know that the others are snug and safe. Even when the snow comes up to the windowsills."

"Well, then, I guess the only thing left to decide is whether the main bedroom is the one on the ground floor, or the one over the living room, with the view over the river and the home fields."

"Oh, the second floor, definitely. Who wouldn't want to wake up to that view? The ground floor bedroom is for guests—older people might have trouble with the stairs. And during church, you know, the young mothers need somewhere to go when the *Bopplin* are fussy."

"Good thinking," he said with admiration. "It's almost as though you've been walking around this meadow with a purpose."

Heat climbed into her cheeks. "I was just guessing. I didn't know for sure and certain that this was your spot."

"I don't think you found it by accident. I think *der Herr* might have given you a nudge. And a vision."

"*Ja*, maybe He did." Her heart sped up as he took a step and linked his hands loosely in the small of her back. His scent—clean cotton and a tang of sweat that told her he hadn't taken his time coming to her—filled her head.

"I have a vision, too," he said in a low tone, his gaze on hers. "I see you in my real house, walking its rooms. Filling them with happiness. Love. I want you in my house, Kate. In my life. You belong here in a way no one else does. But—"

Her heart nearly stopped in its mad gallop. Why was there always a *but*?

"But if you want to wait a year, like you said a few days ago, I'm willing."

"I don't want to. But to give yourself a chance—to be sure—"

"I know it seems crazy and fast and everything I know the two of us are not. But when I crested that ridge up there and saw you walking through the rooms of my house as if it were already real … Kate, I knew. I knew we would make it real. Together."

Joy was rising through her like a lark rising into the sky. And then she remembered.

"But I have to leave on Thursday!"

"Do you really?"

She leaned her forehead on his chest. "Elizabeth wants me to go home with her."

A chuckle sounded in his throat. "We'll see if that actually happens."

"One of us has to go, Adam. Mamm can't manage on her own, not with only my two little sisters to help."

"Then I will talk with Dat about taking a summer job in Whinburg Township. Whether here or there, we'll have a proper courtship."

"Do you mean it?"

"Do you want me to put it in writing?" His dark gaze thrilled her with its humor—and its promise. "That will be my first and last letter to you. At the end, I'll say *I love you, Kate Weaver.* And I promise that when we're old and the floors under our feet right here are worn and scuffed from critters and *Kinner,* I'll hold you just like this and say them once more, still meaning it with all my heart."

Her lips trembled with joy and tears. "I love you, too, Adam Miller. With or without a letter. There's never been anyone for me but you."

When he kissed her, her whole soul promised itself to him. And in the joy of that kiss, neither of them noticed when his hat fell off altogether and landed among the lupines.

Epilogue

THE WESTERN NEWS
Friday, June 11

From Bad Boy to Cowboy
Cord McLean Preps Movie in Lincoln County

Missoula, Montana— Fans of the rodeo circuit had an unexpected surprise this week when Hollywood bad boy Cord McLean, 26-year-old star of last year's Oscar contender *Shadow of My Former Self*, was spotted talking with the buckaroos behind the stands.

"Just doing some onsite research for my next project," he told fans, who promptly wallpapered their Instagram feeds with selfies taken with the popular actor. "If you've ever read the 1940s novel *Ride Forever* by mystery novelist Lee Bateson, you might remember that it's set on a failing Montana ranch."

When asked how long he planned to stay in Lincoln County, the actor was quick to say, "Not long this time. But I'll be back in August for cowboy training." He'll be playing the part of George Reece, the cowboy figure many scholars of Western literature believe was based on Lee Bateson's father Franklin, who never met his son in real life. "I'll be up in the Siksika near a little place called Mountain Home, learning to rope and ride. As you know, I do all my own stunts, so I'm planning on a month of physical training and preparation. Certainly not enough to compete with these guys here, but enough to do justice to Bateson's book and to the script."

So no showing his skill at the Lincoln County Fair in August? "Probably not," the actor said with a laugh. "If I can manage not to shame my trainers, I'll be satisfied." When asked where he would be training, the actor declined to answer. "I want to respect the family's privacy," he said. "But safe to say that they have a sterling reputation for horsemanship and are one of the most successful ranches in Montana. I'm honored they've accepted the challenge, and I'm really looking forward to becoming part of ranch life there."

Since McLean has a reputation for serial engagements and is a staple on the party circuit, a month on a working Montana ranch will definitely be a new experience for him. Readers and fans in the county will be able to see the results when *Ride Forever* releases in October of next year.

———

MAMM LOOKED up as Malena set a cup of coffee down next to the paper, then slid into her own chair with her cup. Across from her,

Rebecca made kissing noises in little Deborah's neck, making the baby grin and wave her hands.

"It seems so quiet here with Adam and Kate and Elizabeth gone," Malena mused. "I'm missing them already. Two of them, anyway."

"That girl is going to be sorry she turned up her nose at your quilt pattern," Rebecca said. Rebecca, who was the most forgiving persona Malena knew, had not quite recovered from those five fateful seconds when Elizabeth had first seen the Mariner's Compass pattern made so carefully for her. When Kate had shown it to her, and explained that she planned to make it for a belated twenty-first birthday gift now that the wedding was off, Malena had seen Elizabeth hesitate. She'd recovered, of course, and said that it was every bit as beautiful as the one at Bylers', but Malena had seen the truth.

The quilt pattern was flawed somehow, and even if she had the skill to fix it, Kate wouldn't let her.

"I'm going to save this for myself," she'd told Malena privately, later. "I know my sister. If it's not exactly what she has in her head, she won't be happy. This pattern makes me happy, so I'm going to make it for my own wedding day."

Which had made Malena feel a lot better.

To change the subject now, she indicated the newspaper article with a lift of her chin. "Looks like the news is out."

"The who and the why, maybe," Mamm said, her gaze falling on the headline once again. "But not the where. For which we can only be thankful."

"How long do the Madisons think they can keep this a secret?" Malena wondered aloud. "I'm surprised Trey and Chance haven't blabbed the news about their famous house guest all over creation, and used it in an advertising campaign on the Rocking Diamond's website, to boot."

"It can't be long," Rebecca said. "Once they gave out the name of our town, it's only the process of elimination before the papers figure out it's the Rocking Diamond. And then what? Are we going to be overrun with autograph hunters instead of the regular kind?"

"Let's hope not," Mamm said with a shudder.

"I'm glad Adam is coming back in August. If our hands have to spend their days chasing off people instead of coyotes, I want all my boys home."

"And Rebecca probably wants hers home," Malena said slyly.

"Until August, Noah has his work to finish, and I have mine," her twin said mildly, refusing to rise to the bait. "But I hope Kate comes back with Adam. At the very least, I think she should spend Christmas with us."

"*Gut* idea," Mamm said. "When the time comes, I'll invite her."

"And Elizabeth?" Malena asked, though of course she knew the answer.

"If Mark Yoder hasn't learned his lesson and proposed again by then, he'll miss a real good opportunity," Mamm said with a laugh. "I almost didn't believe it when she actually got on that bus yesterday. I thought for sure and certain Andrew would prevent it somehow, after all the fuss he's made over her the past week."

"I'm sure the word will get back to Mark and

he'll soon see the error of his ways," Rebecca said.

Malena was silent. Having Elizabeth Weaver as a house guest, with the constant stream of young men and the complete change in the spirit of the doings among the *Youngie*, had been a shock to the system. How had Kate stood it all these years? The more she thought about it, the more it seemed a miracle that Gott had brought Kate and Adam together, and allowed them to see past the bright sun that was Elizabeth to the reality of their own love.

Lord, when will it be my turn?

For while it brought joy and tears to see her siblings find the partner that *Gott* wanted for them, the fact remained that it hurt to be the one still waiting. Did Zach feel the same? Probably not. And if he did, he'd never say so. No, it was just her, Malena, feeling sorry for herself … and feeling far more relief than she should that Elizabeth Weaver had gone back to Pennsylvania where she belonged.

"Anybody want to cut out this article for their scrapbook?"

Mamm's idea of a joke. She folded it up and held out her arms for Deborah.

"*Neh*," Malena said, getting up to clear the table of the coffee things. "Whatever is going on at the Rocking Diamond has nothing to do with us."

THE END

Afterword
A NOTE FROM ADINA

I hope you've enjoyed the fourth book about the Miller family. If you subscribe to my newsletter, you'll hear about new releases in the series, my research in Montana, and snippets about quilting and writing and chickens—my favorite subjects! I hope you'll join me by subscribing at www.subscribepage.com/shelley-adina

And I invite you to visit my online store, www.moonshellbooks.com

While you're there, be sure to browse my other Amish novels set in beautiful Whinburg Township, Pennsylvania, beginning with *The Wounded Heart.*

Afterword

To find out what happens when Cord McLean lands on the Rocking Diamond, I hope you'll go on to the fifth book in the Montana Millers series, *The Amish Cowboy's Makeover*. Here's a sneak peek! —Adina

---

The Amish Cowboy's Makeover
© 2023 Adina Senft

God specializes in makeovers.
—*Mountain Home Amish proverb*

Vibrant, laughing, and with a *wunderbaar* gift of quilt design from God, Malena Miller is always in the middle of the doings among the Amish *Youngie* in Mountain Home, Montana. And there are big doings on the Rocking Diamond, the *Englisch* dude ranch next door to the Circle M. When Malena and her brothers are offered jobs helping a movie star learn how to be a cowboy for his upcoming picture, Malena wonders if her father's silence and her mother's worry are worth the generous salary.

Afterword

And then there's Cord McLean, the actor, who definitely prefers her teaching methods to anyone else's.

Alden Stolzfus has been sweet on Malena ever since his family moved to the valley, but he's too shy to tell her the truth in his heart. It hurts to watch this Hollywood bad boy gradually work his way closer to Malena, under the guise of learning about ranch life. If Cord is getting a makeover to turn him into a cowboy, then maybe Alden had better take a hard look at himself, too.

All the bashful blacksmith has to do is make himself over … and become the hero of her dreams.

The Montana Millers. They believe in faith, family, and the land. They'll need all three when love comes to the Circle M!

Look for The Amish Cowboy's Makeover on my store at moonshellbooks.com, or on your favorite online retailer!

Glossary

Spelling and definitions from Eugene S. Stine, *Pennsylvania German Dictionary* (Birdboro, PA: Pennsylvania German Society, 1996).

Words used:
    alt Maedel old maid
    batzich crazy
    Bohnesuppe bean soup
    Boppli(n) baby, babies
    Bruder, mei my brother
    Herr, der the Lord
    Daadi Haus grandfather house
    denki thank you

Glossary

dochsder(e) daughter(s)
druwwel trouble
Duchly headscarf
Englisch non-Amish people, the English language
Fraa, mei my wife
Freinde friend
Gmay congregation
Gott God
guder owed, wie geht's? good afternoon, how's it going?
gut good
Himmel heaven
hochmut proud
Ischt okay? Is it okay?
ja yes
Kaffee coffee
Kapp prayer covering worn by Amish women
Kinner children
Kumm mit. Come with me.
lieber Vater in Himmel dear Father in Heaven
Liebling darling
Maedel young girl
maedscher young girls

Middaagesse midday meal
Narr idiot
neh no
nix is it not, colloq. ain't so
Neuwesitzer lit. side-sitter, or bridal supporter
Rumspringe The time of running around for Amish youth
Schwei sister-in-law
schweschder(e) sister, sisters
Sohn, mei my son
Vater father
Vorsinger person who starts the hymns in church
Was ischt, Mamm? What is it, Mom?
wilkumm welcome
wille will
wunderbaar wonderful
Youngie young people

Also by Adina Senft

Amish Cowboys of Montana
The Amish Cowboy's Christmas prequel novella
The Amish Cowboy
The Amish Cowboy's Baby
The Amish Cowboy's Bride
The Amish Cowboy's Letter
The Amish Cowboy's Makeover
The Amish Cowboy's Home
The Amish Cowboy's Refuge
The Amish Cowboy's Mistake
The Amish Cowboy's Little Matchmakers
The Amish Cowboy's Wedding Quilt
The Amish Cowboy's Journey

The Whinburg Township Amish

The Wounded Heart

The Hidden Life

The Tempted Soul

Herb of Grace

Keys of Heaven

Balm of Gilead

The Longest Road

The Highest Mountain

The Sweetest Song

The Heart's Return (novella)

———

Breaking Faith

Grounds to Believe

Pocketful of Pearls

Sounds in the Night

Over Her Head

———

Glory Prep (faith-based young adult)

Glory Prep

The Fruit of My Lipstick

Be Strong and Curvaceous

Who Made You a Princess?

Tidings of Great Boys

The Chic Shall Inherit the Earth

About the Author

USA Today bestselling author Adina Senft grew up in a plain house church, where she was often asked by outsiders if she was Amish (the answer was no). She holds a PhD in Creative Writing from Lancaster University in the UK. Adina was the winner of RWA's RITA Award for Best Inspirational Novel in 2005 for *Grounds to Believe*, a finalist for that award in 2006 for *Pocketful of Pearls*, and was a Christy Award finalist in 2009 for *The Fruit of My Lipstick*. She appeared in the 2016 documentary film *Love Between the Covers*, is a popular speaker and convention panelist, and has been a guest on many podcasts, including Worldshapers and Realm of Books.

She writes steampunk adventure and mystery as Shelley Adina; and as Charlotte Henry, writes classic Regency romance. When she's not writing, Adina is usually quilting, sewing historical costumes, or enjoying the garden with her flock of rescued chickens.

Adina loves to talk with readers about books, quilting, and chickens!
www.moonshellbooks.com

- facebook.com/adinasenft
- pinterest.com/shelleyadina
- bookbub.com/authors/adina-senft
- instagram.com/shelleyadinasenft
- bsky.app/profile/shelleyadinasenft.bsky.social

Made in the USA
Middletown, DE
13 February 2025

71303074R00217